"I beg your pardon," snapped Alexandria.

"You heard me right. Will you marry me?"

"Your idea of humor is really quite reprehensible, Mr. Romney. Now, if you'll excuse me. . ." Alexandria wheeled to leave.

"Alex, damn it all, be sensible," he said, holding her wrist. "I'm offering you a way out of the coil you've landed in. I want something else from you far more than I desire a dowry."

Her own eyes widened with a nervousness she tried to hide. "Oh, and what could that be?"

"My freedom."

By Marian Devon
Published by Fawcett Books:

MISS ARMSTEAD WEARS BLACK GLOVES
MISS ROMNEY FLIES TOO HIGH
M'LADY RIDES FOR A FALL
SCANDAL BROTH
SIR SHAM
A QUESTION OF CLASS
ESCAPADE
FORTUNES OF THE HEART
MISS OSBORNE MISBEHAVES
LADY HARRIET TAKES CHARGE
MISTLETOE AND FOLLY
A SEASON FOR SCANDAL
A HEART ON HIS SLEEVE
AN UNCIVIL SERVANT
DEFIANT MISTRESS
THE WIDOW OF BATH
THE ROGUE'S LADY

THE ROGUE'S LADY

Marian Devon

FAWCETT CREST • NEW YORK

A Fawcett Crest Book
Published by Ballantine Books
Copyright © 1982 by Marian Pope Rettke

Originally published by The Berkley/Jove Publishing Group in 1982.

ISBN 0-449-21668-3

Manufactured in the United States

First Ballantine Books Edition: June 1995

10 9 8 7 6 5 4 3 2

Chapter One

THE HONORABLE HENRY ROMNEY WAS EAVESDROP-
ping. That Harry made no attempt to disguise
his ungentlemanly behavior did not surprise Miss
Alexandria Linnell, who watched from across the
room. She might, though, have been surprised to
learn that she was the subject of his interest.

Seated dutifully next to Lady Augusta, who was
sound asleep, either lulled by or escaping from the
tunes being pounded into the pianoforte, Alexandria had been watching Harry for some time now.
She needed the distraction. For she did not dare
fasten her attention where it belonged, upon the
young lady across the gold withdrawing room who
was attacking the piano keys with more determina-
tion than artistic skill, grimly accompanying her
own off-key soprano. More particularly, Alexandria
did not dare look upon the handsome, fair-haired

young man who was turning the pages for her. And so she watched Harry Romney as an escape and almost forgot her misery in her amusement at his boredom.

Why he had come to this gathering, convened for the sole purpose of introducing Sir Oliver Linnell's affianced bride to his relations, she could not imagine. Harry Romney had never been possessed of any general family feeling, and he disliked his cousin Oliver in particular. Alexandria surmised that his was a command appearance. He'd arrived late, in the midst of dinner, wearing skintight trousers and varnished boots, and had joined the company at the first remove without bothering to change to the requisite knee smalls for evening wear. Nor had he rectified this sartorial solecism after dinner. His coat of bright blue superfine stood out garishly among the proper blacks and whites of his more conventional male relatives. But if he was even conscious of the contrast, he did not show it.

Alexandria had watched him keep his eyes upon the performer for a while. But there was little about Lady Amelia to hold his interest for very long. She was a nondescript young lady. Those features that claimed attention did so mainly for their defects, such as small grey eyes with a slight tendency to cast and a nose rather too prominent for any claim to charm. And since Harry's tastes, so Alexandria had been told, ran to beauties of the more flamboyant style, opera dancers in particular, and since her fortune held no charms for him, only her performance could hope to win him. Alexandria had almost giggled as she saw him flinch at a grating, wavering high note. She would never have taken the Honorable Henry for a music lover. But he obviously had an ear.

He had then shifted his position slightly to lean indolently against the Adam-style fireplace and let his dark eyes wander throughout the room. He caught Alexandria watching him and raised an eyebrow, but otherwise his harsh face betrayed nothing but its usual boredom while he tallied the dozen or so Linnell relations, most of whom wore glazed expressions of endurance as Oliver's intended entertained.

Harry seemed to find little to inspire in the sight of his gathered kin. They ranged from their ancient sleeping hostess, Oliver's grandmother and Harry's own great-aunt, on down to young Horatio Linnell, ten years old, who was kicking his heels distractedly against the gold paint decoration of a Hepplewhite elbow chair while his mother glared impotently from a distance. But then the Honorable Henry's attention had fastened upon two lace-capped cousins deep in whispered conversation, and he had moved over behind the gossipmongers to hear more easily. He need not have bothered to change his position, for at that moment the music shifted to pianissimo and caught the conversation in midstride.

". . . should have kept to her room as befits her station." The stage whisper would have done credit to the great actor Garrick. So well did it travel across the room to where Alexandria and her employer sat that she had no hope it had escaped the ears of anyone. "Shows a decided want of conduct on her part," the speaker went on to say. "Most improper!"

"But that's not fair. She is still family." The second speaker was more charitable but no less audible. "Besides, I dare say poor Alexandria had no choice at all in the matter. It was all Augusta's doing, mark my words. You know perfectly well she's always loved to stir up mischief. And age makes her worse, not better. She obviously wanted to embarrass dear Oliver, not to mention . . ." Here, mercifully, the soprano swelled to an ear-splitting crescendo as Alexandria felt her face flame hot, a condition that was not aided by Harry Romney's wicked grin in her direction.

"I want my tea!" Perhaps Lady Augusta had heard her name. At any rate something roused her from sleep and she raised her turbaned head to make the stentorian announcement as the music quavered to a graceless close and everyone, with the exception of the Honorable Henry, clapped politely.

Servants, who had anticipated Lady Augusta by several minutes and were poised outside the door, rolled in the tea cart, heavily laden with fruits and cheeses, cold meats and seed cake, and placed it near the center of the room, where it acted as a magnet for the music-weary guests.

"I want my tea now, Alexandria!" the dowager demanded once again, and her young companion rose reluctantly to fetch it. The reluctance stemmed not from a flagging sense of duty, but from the awareness that Sir Oliver, relieved of his duty as page-turner, was now busily pouring tea for the performer. And walk slowly as she might, Alexandria realized, she was bound to arrive at the tea tray under the curious eyes of all their family before her cousin left it.

One member of the company, however, was not content merely to watch the embarrassing reunion.

The Honorable Henry timed his own trip in order to encounter both of them there, a situation that would have earned Alexandria's gratitude if she had thought for one minute that Harry had acted from a sense of diplomacy rather than of mischief.

Indeed his intent was soon obvious. When Oliver murmured self-consciously, "How are you, Alexandria?" while he poured out tea with a hand not entirely steady, Harry leaped in uninvited to answer for her.

"Why, she's obviously blooming," he replied. "I'm frankly amazed, Alex, that you turned out so well. I would have wagered almost anything against your becoming such a beauty. You really were a most scruffy child, as I recall."

"Then your powers of recollection are quite poor," Oliver replied haughtily. "Alexandria has always been attractive."

"Really?" His cousin's dark eyebrows shot up in mock surprise. "We surely can't both be talking about the same skinny child who was all eyes and teeth."

Oliver was not amused, but Alexandria acknowledged the truth of the unflattering description with a smile. Harry too had changed since she'd last seen him in his youth. He hadn't been so tall, of course, and though his expression had been cynical even then, his face had had some vestiges of childish softness. Now it seemed all hard planes and angles, in swarthy contrast to Oliver's fair good looks. Nor had his nose been quite so hawk-like, she thought critically. He was a boxer, come to think of it, so Oliver had once told her, one of the rackety set of young aristocrats who liked to step into the ring with Cribb and Belcher, the Terrible

Randall, and other professionals. No doubt he'd had his nose broken there.

"Actually," Harry was remarking thoughtfully to his seething cousin, "I suppose that even now it's coming it a bit strong to call Alexandria beautiful." She might have been a china ornament he was discussing with such detachment as he picked up a plate and began to pile it high. "Though I do think those eyes might qualify now that the face has finally caught up and she's lost her baby-owl look. They are the clearest, truest blue I've seen in quite some time. But otherwise she really doesn't have much claim to be called a beauty. Attractive, certainly. But I should not have used 'beauty' so readily, I think, if it had not been for present company. Any fairly presentable woman here would suddenly seem a stunner. Take your fiancée for instance, my dear fellow," he continued thoughtfully as Oliver's cheeks turned red. " 'Platter-faced' is putting it quite charitably. And I really don't see how you can bear those wandering eyes, even for nine thousand pounds a year."

"Damn you, you never change! How dare you—" Oliver choked out the words as he snatched up his betrothed's tea things. "How you can speak so slightingly of a lady so far above your touch— whose countenance, I might add, most people find quite pleasing—"

"Do they, by Jove?" his cousin answered with some surprise. "Well, there's never any accounting for taste, is there? Though I will say this much," he added glumly. "She certainly is preferable to her sister."

Alexandria, following his gaze to where Lady Arabel Fielding had joined her elder sister on a

6

striped love seat, thought that he was right. Amelia was the more attractive of the two, possibly because there was less of her. Harry Romney did not try to repress a shudder as he took in Lady Arabel's plump face, broadened even further by clusters of fat curls dangling before her ears. "But at least she doesn't sing," he remarked charitably. Alexandria involuntarily let out a giggle and the enraged Oliver turned on his heel and left them.

"You really should be ashamed of yourself," Alexandria said, sounding like the governess she once had been, "speaking so shabbily of the two Lady Fieldings to Oliver."

"Hypocrite," Harry rejoined carelessly. "You enjoyed every minute of it."

"Alexandria!" Lady Augusta hallooed from across the room. "Stop talking to that scrapegrace and fetch my tea!"

"I have it, Aunt Augusta," Mr. Romney shouted back. "I feared that Miss Linnell was too frail to carry a sufficient supply for you." He took the plate he'd been filling and a cup of tea and headed for the dowager while Alexandria unloaded two-thirds of the provisions she'd accumulated and, ignoring the glances of her kin, trailed after him.

"What brings you up north, Harry? Did I invite you?" Lady Augusta shouted as Mr. Romney pulled up a chair beside the sofa she and Alexandria occupied.

"My father seemed to think so. At least he said that the entire family had received your royal summons."

"Humph. Knew I hadn't asked you. Wouldn't have thought you'd have much in common with this gaggle of Linnells." The old lady chuckled as if

7

she'd made a joke and shot him a sideways malicious glance from under drooping eyelids. "You don't take much after your Linnell relations, do you, boy?" She laughed uproariously.

Harry gave the cackling crone a level look. "Oh, don't you think so? My enemies say I get my spiteful tongue from you."

Alexandria waited for the explosion that was sure to follow. Instead, the old lady seemed delighted. "Spiteful like me, eh? Well, I still know a thing or two, I'll tell you that much. And I know you didn't ride up here to wish your cousin Oliver happy. You never could abide him when you were small—regular little prig you thought him; and of course you were a limb of Satan—and I doubt you've changed your mind about him. By the by," she changed her tack suddenly, "what do you mean by coming to my table dressed like a cit? Why didn't you change to evening clothes?"

"For the same reason you haven't changed that ghastly purple turban in a decade. It didn't suit me."

"Outrageous!" The dowager reached over and rapped her young male relative on the knuckles with her ivory fan. With some satisfaction Alexandria noted that Harry winced.

"As I was saying," the old lady took up her main conversational thread again, "I couldn't imagine why you came here. But then it hit me all of a sudden. Woolridge must be pushing you at the younger Fielding."

"My father did encourage me to meet her," Harry admitted.

"Your father's an ass."

"Out of filial respect, I'll pretend I never heard that," he replied.

"Fustian! You've called him worse to his face, I'll wager. Why ain't he here, by the by? He's the one with proper family feeling."

"Parliament's in session and the fate of the empire rides on his being there."

Alexandria was beginning to feel that she wasn't really there at all. But after two disastrous attempts at being a governess and six only slightly more successful months as a companion, she had grown almost accustomed to being socially ignored. Now she took advantage of the conversation which swirled around her to sneak a look at Oliver across the way. Then she wished that she had not, as she saw his handsome head bent in rapt attention to the chatter of his bride-to-be.

"I hear Woolridge hopes to be Prime Minister," Lady Augusta was saying to her nephew. "That is, if you don't throw a rub in his way by finally landing in one scrape too many. They tell me you're better known than he is, with your gambling and your brawling and your Cyprians."

"Oh, I think 'they' exaggerate," Harry replied lazily.

"That's as may be. But if Woolridge thinks he'll straighten you out by coupling you with that Fielding chit, he's gone queer in the attic is what I think."

"If you say so."

"I do say so. She ain't your style at all. It's well enough for Oliver to marry an ugly girl. He needs the blunt. But they say old Flynn left you plump in the pocket, a regular nabob, in fact. That true?"

"More or less."

"Rummest thing I ever heard of—an Irishman with money. Even rummer that he left it all to you. But under the circumstances, it's downright pudding-headed of Woolridge to think of you marrying that fat Fielding girl. Why, she's worse than her sister."

"Just what I told Oliver."

"You didn't!" The old lady cackled delightedly while Alexandria looked disapproving. Unfortunately, the dowager noticed her expression. "Don't look so Friday-faced, missy. It's time you stopped concerning yourself with your cousin Oliver. He's above your touch now and that's a fact. And don't think that just because I've been conversing with this rogue that I haven't noticed you making sheep's eyes in Oliver's direction. I wish you'd pay half as much attention to me as you do to Oliver. Then you'd see that I'm like to take a chill from sitting in this draft and run to fetch my shawl."

"I'll get it right away." Alexandria placed her half-empty tea cup on the rosewood sofa table and stood up.

"Finish your tea first," the old lady said grudgingly.

"I've had quite enough, thank you," Alexandria answered, not really meaning tea, and hurried off to get the shawl.

It took some time, however, to find the elusive garment. She finally spied it behind Lady Augusta's immense four-poster bed and was coming back down the stairs when she was waylaid by Harry Romney.

"I need to talk to you," he said abruptly.

"Then why didn't you merely wait? You knew I must be right back."

"I mean privately. Come outside with me."

She gave him a speaking look. "You surely cannot have forgotten that I'm on an errand."

"Oh, the shawl. She won't miss it. She's popped off to sleep again. But if it will ease your conscience, I'll go drape it over the harridan. Superfluous though. She's got enough gall to keep her warm." He reached out to take the woolen garment, but Alexandria held on to it.

"Mr. Romney," she began with dignity.

"Good God! What has happened to 'Harry'? Or to 'odious creature,' for that matter?"

"Mr. Romney, surely you must be aware of my position." Alexandria tried unsuccessfully to keep the bitterness from her voice. "I'm no longer Miss Linnell of Rose Hall, but a hired companion. A wage earner."

"And a low enough wage at that, I've no doubt, knowing the old clutch-penny. Yes, I know all about your father losing the family fortune. And about the gallant Oliver terminating your betrothal."

"You much mistake the matter. We were not betrothed," she replied icily.

"No? Well, you'll not deny there was an understanding—but don't fly off into the boughs again. I'll drop the subject. But I still need to talk to you. Get your cloak and come outside."

"As I was attempting to explain, even if I were inclined to go outside with you, which I certainly am not, my present status would not permit it. Such behavior would cost me my position. It doesn't even bear thinking of."

"No? I wonder if you'd think of it if the fair-haired Oliver were to ask you?" he inquired.

Instead of replying, Alexandria attempted to

walk past him down the stairs, but he grabbed her arm and held her fast. "That remark was uncalled for and I regret it. But, all the same, I must talk to you on a matter of some importance. If not now, when? Could you contrive to slip out after the old battle-ax is tucked in bed?"

She gave him a quelling look. "Mr. Romney," she began impatiently.

"All right, then. Don't read me a lecture. Just tell me when I can see you alone."

Alexandria began to waver as she detected some urgency in his voice. "Perhaps in the morning, before Lady Augusta is out of bed."

"My God, when is that?" No early riser, Mr. Romney looked appalled.

"Would daybreak suit?" she asked mischievously.

"I suppose it will have to," he groaned.

"Confound that girl, where is she?" came a querulous voice floating up the stairs, overriding completely the hum of conversations and the clink of cups. "I want my shawl."

"Daybreak, then. In the maze. That should keep us from prying eyes," Harry said quickly before Alexandria could bolt past him down the stairs.

"Very well. If it's truly urgent."

"It's urgent, all right. A matter of life and death, in fact."

She paused a moment on the bottom step and looked up at him, wide-eyed. "You can't be serious."

"Never more so in my life. We have to prevent a murder."

"A murder! Whose?" she gasped.

"Lady Augusta's. A few more days of fetch and carry and I wouldn't give any odds at all against your doing the old devil in."

"Alexandria!" The voice increased in volume.

"Run on then, girl." Harry gave a dismissive wave. "Wrap the old nag in her horse blanket. In the meantime, I'll lock up the knives and hide all the blunt instruments. Just try and contain yourself till morning."

Chapter
Two

*L*ADY AUGUSTA WAS IN A JOVIAL MOOD AS ALEXANDRIA helped her settle for the night. When the companion drew a chair near the lamp on the bedside table and prepared to read *Belinda*, which so far had never failed to put her ladyship to sleep, the dowager waved the book away. "I want to talk," she said. "Fetch me a glass of port."

Alexandria rose obediently and poured the wine from a bottle kept conveniently on the clothes press floor. The old lady smacked her lips over it, then looked sideways at Alexandria. "Well, speak up, girl. What do you think of her?"

"Of whom?" Alexandria replied.

" 'Of whom,' " the other mimicked. "Of Oliver's young woman, that's 'of whom'. Who else would we be talking of? Come on, say it. What do you think of her?"

Alexandria rose with all the dignity she could muster. "Lady Augusta, if you have no further need of me, I should like to retire. I have the headache."

"Hoity-toity. Aren't we on the high ropes, though? Sit down, miss. Well, then, we won't discuss Lady Amelia if you haven't a mind to, though I will say, if Oliver's going to have to listen to that caterwauling for the rest of his life, the poor boy will earn his nine thousand pounds and no mistake. I vow, if she'd sung just one more stanza it would not have surprised me to see him snatch you by the hand and run for Gretna Green, pauper or not." She cackled wickedly. "Now sit down, Alexandria, till I dismiss you. My, my, we are touchy, are we not? Very well. I'll change the subject. Only, did you hear that rascal Harry call her ugly?"

"I heard you call her that and he agreed. Actually his term was 'platter-faced.'"

Lady Augusta clapped hands delightedly. "Platter-faced! Damme, he's right. And I'll bet a monkey he threw the term right in Oliver's teeth. He always did love to bait his cousin."

"Harry Romney's ill manners were never confined just to Oliver, as I recall."

"Maybe not. But you must have noticed that there was something about Oliver that always brought out the worst in Harry. Remember when they were boys and Oliver had a new white suit? No, you would have been too small. He looked like a little cherub," she smiled fondly at the memory, "with his plump little face and lovely blue eyes and his golden curls. And, of course, everyone went into raptures over him. But I could tell that none of it sat well with Master Romney. And it crossed my mind that he was plotting some kind of mischief.

"Jealous, of course. No matter how they dressed him up, in five minutes' time Harry always looked like a chimney sweep." She chuckled. "Sure enough, before the morning was half over, Oliver was covered from head to toe in muck. Oliver claimed that Harry pushed him. Of course the rascal said his cousin slipped."

Alexandria looked disgusted. "Oliver was right, then. Harry has not changed."

"No, nor ever will, I suspect. He's certainly a thorn in Woolridge's flesh." The old lady shook her head in mock despair. "Pity Oliver wasn't his son instead. But I must say I've always liked the scamp. Shame he's not a Romney. If he was, I'd think better of the line. Never could stomach that family. Too high in the instep with too little reason for it, was my opinion. Said as much to Oliver's father when he got himself engaged to Woolridge's younger sister. 'Can't imagine why you'd want to wed one of those overbred Romneys' is what I said to him straight out."

"But I don't understand." Alexandria looked bewildered. "Whatever do you mean about Henry— Harry—"

"Just what I said, girl. Pay attention. He's not a Romney."

Alexandria looked uneasily at the remaining bit of port in Lady Augusta's glass and wondered about the vintage. It must be of extraordinary potency, she speculated. Her ladyship's mental faculties, usually quite keen, seemed suddenly adrift.

"I'm not foxed, if that's what you're thinking." The dowager obviously could read her mind. "I'm surprised you didn't know it. That Harry's not Woolridge's son, I mean. It was the *on-dit* of London a few years ago. But I suppose the talk's died down now. And certainly neither of those two would admit it, even with pistols held to their heads. Especially not Woolridge. But just the same, it's common knowledge that Harry is a bastard. Had to be. For one thing, Lydia Flynn—she was Harry's mother, you know. Beautiful woman. Too bad he got his wildness from her and not his looks. But, to get back to the point, Lydia Flynn always had men swarming after her like bees for honey. And there was that Lieutenant O'Hara in particular—a rackety Irish cousin—who was dangling after her some nine months before Harry came along. That was enough to make society suspicious.

"Then Harry turned out to be an only child. Looks nothing like Woolridge either. You must have noticed that. And the boy don't favor the Flynns at all. But as if those facts weren't sufficient to start the tongues to wagging, folk couldn't help but notice that when Lydia Flynn died and Woolridge remarried, he never produced any offspring on his second trip to the well."

"Why, Harry has two or three half-brothers—sisters—whatever," Lady Augusta's shocked companion intervened.

"They ain't Woolridge's. All from his lady's first marriage." The old woman sounded like a barrister summing up his case.

"But really," Alexandria protested, disgusted by her employer's coarseness. "Just because Lord Woolridge had only one son is hardly reason to think—"

"Not think, know," Lady Augusta snorted. "Why do you suppose Woolridge has treated the boy the way he has all these years? He could never bear the sight of Harry. And if you ask me, that's what's made Harry such a hellion. But anyhow"— she drained the dregs of the glass and smacked her lips over it—"he has the Romney name. And Woolridge wants the name to live. And that's his only chance. I'll wager that Harry, at least, has the seed for it." She gave a salacious chuckle. "I don't doubt he's proved it more than once by now. No need to look so missish, Alexandria. That's the trouble with your generation. You're always romanticizing. Ought to look at life the way it is. Spend some time in the stables or the barnyard. Learn what's what. Too much poetry reading, that's the trouble with you young people nowadays. Filled with romantic rubbish. If instead of reading all that flummery together, you had simply lured Oliver into a hay rick and had a few good tumbles with him, he'd not be planning now to wed that Fielding prig, who'll no doubt swoon at the first sight of him without his nightshirt.

"Oh, very well then, miss. Go on to your bed." She waved her hand in dismissal as Alexandria rose protestingly to her feet. "But fill my glass before you go. It looks like a long night ahead. Much too keyed up to sleep. Might as well make the most of it."

Several hours later, as she tossed and turned upon her bed, Alexandria wished she'd helped herself to the port as well. She would have welcomed its numbing properties. Like her employer, she was too keyed up to have a hope of sleeping. And much too miserable. The scene in the withdrawing room had been hard enough to bear. She needed only to close her eyes for the image of Oliver dancing attendance upon his future bride to reappear. But a later encounter had been even more unsettling. She had been sent back downstairs to hunt for Lady Augusta's ever elusive shawl and had returned with it just in time to see Oliver gravely bidding his betrothed good night at her bedchamber door. The sorrowful gaze he bent on Alexandria behind Lady Amelia's back had made it quite, quite clear that, though he was honorably pledged to do his duty, his heart was breaking for it.

For just a moment the look had warmed her heart. But of course Alexandria could not be comforted for long by Oliver's misery. She loved him far too much to wish him to suffer as she was suffering, she told herself. But somehow, in midthought, the image of Harry Romney rose, giving her a level look and saying "hypocrite."

Suddenly it was all too much to bear. She burst into unaccustomed tears and cried herself to sleep.

Her face next morning betrayed that lapse in her usual stoicism. Since her father's death, followed closely by the realization of her impoverished state, she had held her head erect with the inbred pride of a family that traced its antecedents back to the Conqueror and had defied anyone to catch her indulging in self-pity. Now, as she gazed dolefully at her reddened eyelids reflected in the looking glass, her hope that they'd not betray her to Harry Romney was faint indeed.

He'd been right, she thought as she scrutinized herself, when he'd said her eyes were her only claim to beauty. She found her features regular enough but considered her face a bit too long and her mouth a bit too large for beauty. As for her hair, it was a nondescript light brown. Of course it was quite plentiful and it was possessed of a nice sheen that almost, not quite, redeemed it. Still, only her eyes could be called extraordinary, and now they were bloodshot and rimmed by puffy eyelids.

Well, she had no need to impress the Honorable Henry Romney. Or anybody else for that matter. Besides, Harry was known for self-centeredness. Perhaps he'd be too concerned with whatever he felt he must discuss with her to notice her ravaged countenance.

She held the thought as she donned her pattens and her heavy cloak, preparing to go out into the blustery January morning that threatened rain, or worse, at any moment. Why they could not meet in a civilized manner at breakfast, where a fire would be crackling in the fireplace, was more than she could say. Trust Harry to make an intrigue out of nothing, she thought peevishly, recalling the childhood games of spies and pirates that he had invariably dreamed up, to her and Oliver's discomfort. She pulled her hood as low as possible, seeking to shadow her tear-blotched face, and stepped outside.

An icy wind caught Alexandria's cloak and undid her careful work by blowing her hood back and whipping her hair loose from the severe coil she'd brushed it into. She raced down the gravel path that led from the south entrance of the house to the formal garden that Lady Augusta still insisted upon maintaining in spite of the modern trend toward natural landscaping. At least the high hedges offered shelter from the wind, she noted, as she ran into the entrance of the maze. Here she paused a moment to push her hair back underneath her hood and thereby regain a bit of dignity.

Then she began cautiously to wend her way through the half-forgotten puzzle. After backtracking only a time or two, she suddenly emerged from the final tortuous twist to find Harry Romney walking up and down impatiently in the center. He was clad in a curly brimmed beaver and a many-caped greatcoat whose well-cut elegance made one forget that it was also created to defy the worst the weather had to offer.

"It's about time," he said impatiently. "I thought you'd lost yourself. I only now remembered how, when we all came here as children, the only way you made it through was when we played Ariadne and guided you with string. If I had recalled that sooner, I'd have met you at the entrance and led you here myself."

"I was not lost," she answered, not quite truthfully. "Now, rather than being so insulting, you might just tell me why you dragged me out here in the cold, then let me get back to my employer."

Instead of answering, he reached over and pushed back her hood. He then backed off and squinted like an artist at her face. "You've been crying." It sounded like an accusation. "I can only hope it's because that harpy Lady Augusta has been beating you again."

"Don't be silly. You know Lady Augusta does no such thing."

"If you've been crying over Oliver, I think a good deal less of you. Frankly, he and Lady Amelia Fielding deserve each other. They are quite well matched, if only he could quit sighing over you long enough to recognize that fact. Not that I did not admire the soulful glances he threw your way when his betrothed's attention was fixed elsewhere. I re-

21

ally feel our Oliver should have gone upon the stage. He has a rare talent for languishing looks. Kemble would die of envy."

Alexandria glared up at him. "I had almost forgot just how despicable you are. But now I recall you as the most odious of boys, who positively enjoyed pulling the wings off flies!"

"Then you remember wrong. Flies and I were on the best of terms. I never troubled them. What you are really recalling is the time I drew your hero Oliver's cork for spoiling the mud fort I'd slaved to build. Are you sure he wasn't your wing-puller, come to think on it? Anyhow, I did bloody his nose that day—which wasn't all that easy, considering you were thumping me with a stick and screaming like a Turk all the time I did so. Good God! You were besotted by him even then, were you not?"

"Surely you did not ask for this assignation to reminisce about our childhood," Alexandria interposed stiffly.

"No, I did not," he answered.

"Then why did you drag me out here on such a morning?"

"Because I wished to find a place that might be clear of our mutual relatives. By the by," he interrupted himself suddenly, "just what sort of cousins are we? Second? Once removed? I never could straighten out our relationship."

"Perhaps that's because we are not related."

"We aren't? Well, you need not sound quite so relieved. It's most uncivil. But are you sure? I could have sworn we were. 'Cousin' Oliver and all of that."

"You are related to him on his mother's side, while he and I are both Linnells."

"Well, then it's the Linnells we've mostly come out here to avoid, since few Romneys were courageous enough to beard Lady Augusta in her den. Anyhow, I dragged you out here, as you ungraciously put it, because I thought a proposal required some privacy. Miss Linnell, will you marry me?"

"I beg your pardon?"

"You heard me right. Will you marry me?"

"Your idea of humor is really quite reprehensible, Mr. Romney. Now, if you'll excuse me, I've duties to attend to." Alexandria wheeled to leave but was prevented from doing so by a vise-like hand upon her wrist.

"Now, wait a minute, Alex. There's no need to get into such a taking. Or to take this as some sort of crude joke on my part either. I'm trying to make you a perfectly serious offer of marriage. Just because I don't go down on one knee and talk the usual romantic rot is no reason for you not to hear me out."

Alexandria made another futile attempt to free herself while Harry's face assumed a pained expression. "I can see now that I really should have thrown in some pre-proposal taradiddle and not rushed headlong to the point. But, damn me, it's cold here. Besides, I've urgent business back in London and want to be on my way. So, to go over it once more, and be sure you get it straight this time—Alex, will you marry me?"

"Don't call me Alex, and no, I won't."

"Dear God, women!" Harry released Alexandria's arm to throw up his hands in helpless frustration. "Here I thought that, under the circumstances, one could dispense with formalities and make a sensible proposal and get a sensible reply. But no. Every female living thinks it's her inalienable right to be wooed first. Alex, damn it all, be sensible. Doesn't it occur to you that I'm offering you a way out of the coil you've landed in?"

"You mean, of course, that I should leap at the chance to wed you."

"Yes, damn it, you should. You can't tell me you enjoy being ordered around like an underservant by that old witch you're companion to. Or that you don't resent having Oliver throw you over to marry a girl whose face would curdle cream. In fact," he added thoughtfully, "if curdled cream is what he's after, she could get the same effect by singing at it. But forget Lady Amelia. Forget both the Fieldings, for that matter. I certainly intend to. To get back to the point, what I'm offering you is a chance to resume your proper station—not to mention an annual income considered by most to be quite handsome. And an eventual title if my father ever decides to quit this vale of tears, which I wouldn't have you count on."

He suddenly began to stamp his gleaming Hessians on the frozen ground. "Damn it, Alex, my feet are frostbit. If you're determined to be missish and coy about all this and want to discuss it further instead of just sensibly agreeing, let's at least walk." So saying, he started briskly back through the maze. "Come on, girl; move before you freeze," he called back over his shoulder to Alexandria, who was already frozen, but more from shock than from the inclement weather. She rallied at his imperious command and came trailing along behind him.

"But why would you wish to marry me?" she inquired of the back of his top cape. He had certainly grown up tall, she thought distractedly. She herself was of average female height, but she'd developed a crick merely from looking up at him. He paused impatiently to let her catch up, then drew her close to walk beside him as her cloak and his greatcoat brushed the hedges in the narrow passage.

"I want to marry you to escape the fatter Fielding," he finally answered.

"But that's absurd. You're twenty-seven and financially independent. You don't have to marry to please your father."

"I don't intend to. Marrying you won't please him. But it will silence him for once and all upon the subject of matrimony. And keep him and every dowager in London from throwing others like the Fielding at my defenseless head."

"My, I never dreamed you were so desirable," Alexandria said with heavy sarcasm as they strode around the end of the particular hedge wall they'd been following.

"Didn't you? Well, you should have done. After Oliver's defection, you should know something of the way the marriage mart works. I'm actually more desirable than his Amelia, if you can imagine such a circumstance, for my income makes hers paltry by comparison."

"As it happens, I do know something of the way the marriage mart is conducted," Miss Linnell retorted. "Enough to realize that nabobs like yourself"—she made the word a mockery—"do not marry paupers. So why me?"

"Simple," he replied as they reached a dead end in the maze and stopped. He turned to face her, his countenance suddenly quite serious, his black eyes boring into hers. "I want something else from you far more than I desire a dowry."

Her own eyes widened with a nervousness she tried to hide. "Oh, and what could that be?" She failed to ask the question lightly.

"My freedom."

"I beg your pardon?"

"Alex, are you hard of hearing? I'm always having to repeat the things I say. I really had not bargained for a wife one has to shout at through an ear trumpet in order to be understood. Not that we will have much to communicate once the knot is tied. Now pay attention. I'm trying to strike a bargain with you. In return for giving you the protection of my name, as the saying goes—which actually means setting up an establishment for you in Grosvenor Square and giving you sufficient allowance to maintain it and yourself—I get the advantage of being a married man, which in my case means a cessation of the lectures by my father on my filial duty and a farewell to all the scheming mamas and their spotty daughters. And I gain the consent of my most tolerant wife"—he gestured in her direction—"to continue leading my life as I've always led it."

"Which means living with the light-skirt of the moment?"

"You've been around Lady Augusta too long already. You're beginning to sound like her." Alexandria reddened at the hit. "But, yes, that among other things," he continued. "Well, what do you say?"

"I say no, of course."

Harry swore, then took Alexandria none too gently by the shoulders and forced her to look at him directly. "By damn, Alex, if you're this stupid, I'm not sure I want you carrying the Romney name. If you're bird-witted enough to turn down an opportunity that would have sent Cinderella leaping out of the ashes to dance a jig just because you don't approve of me and the way I lead my life—or, worse yet, because you're still pining for that clodpole Oliver—you don't deserve—"

"That isn't it at all," she cut him off midtirade. "Of course I see the advantages for me. That's just the point. I can see that for me the marriage would be all you've said and more. What I can't see is why you've suddenly got into such a quixotic taking. Oh, I know." She raised her hand to stop his answering. "I know you believe what you've just said. But I also believe you haven't stopped to think beyond the momentary pleasure you might get from sending your father flying up into the boughs and from . . . from . . ." She groped for the proper word and could not find it. "From annoying Oliver," she finished lamely.

"Well, that's a better beginning than most marriages get off to," he answered cynically. "Come on, Alex." He rubbed his hands together briskly, then blew a cloud of foggy breath onto his numbed fingers. "Say yes and let's go inside."

"I can't," she replied, and this time the regret could no longer be denied. "You're obviously acting upon some sort of impulse you'd soon come to regret. For, as you say, you are extremely eligible. And not bad looking, really." He laughed dryly at the hint of reservation in her tone. "The world of women, even the polite world of women, is not merely populated by the Fielding sisters. You're bound, sooner or later, to meet some well-bred nonpareil and fall in love with her. Then you'd hate yourself *and* me."

He frowned impatiently. "You really are a romantic, Alex, are you not? In spite of Oliver and everything that's happened to you. Stop and think, girl. Just how many love matches have you known of? Your parents, perhaps?"

"Well, no," she admitted honestly. "At least, I do not think so. My mother died when I was ten, of course."

"I assure you they were not," he informed her brutally. "Gambling was not your father's sole addiction. Certainly my father's marriage to my mother would not qualify. And, while his current household is a good deal less stormy, no sane person could consider theirs a love match either. Face it, Alex. At least nine out of ten marriages in Society are marriages of convenience. And ours would be a lot more convenient than most of them. Oh, did I say I would not expect you to—"

"Not exactly," she interrupted quickly, turning pink, "but you rather implied that that part of your life is taken care of."

"Most satisfactorily, in fact. So now what's stopping you? Go give old Augusta your goodbyes and come with me now. I can postpone my business in the metropolis. We can be married by special license."

"No, I'll not come now," she answered slowly. It was obvious that she was capitulating.

"Whyever not?"

"Because I insist upon your taking time to think over what you're doing."

"For God's sake, Alex—oh, very well, then. But it seems unnecessary to make two journeys when one would do. But we'll do it your way. Let's see. Best allow a week—most of which will be spent in travel, but never mind. I'll get here the night before and put up at the Golden Cock. Meet me down at the gatehouse at—oh, Lord, I guess we'd best say daybreak again."

"And if you're not there?"

"I'll be there."

"But if you're not—and I certainly expect you to change your mind—I shall doubtless cause some talk, packing up my possessions and dragging them down to the gate just for an airing."

"No need for that." He looked her expertly up and down. "I can outfit you. It's settled then. Walk down to the gatehouse at first light one week from today. And if I'm not there—though of course I shall be—and someone sees you, you're simply out for a breath of air. You've only to turn around again and walk back home—no questions asked."

"And if I'm not there?" She asked it more for pride's sake than for lack of resolution.

"Then I shall know that you're a hopeless fool and that I've made a trip for nothing. Well, by Jove, not necessarily," he added, brightening up. "Jake the groom was saying there's a new rat pit just opened near the village. So if you are gudgeon enough to get cold feet, at least my journey back up here won't be a total waste."

Chapter Three

"**H**SSST! ALEXANDRIA!"

She had entered the house alone, the Honorable Henry having gone on to the stables to order his curricle for immediate departure. She had prudently come up the back stairs to avoid any other early risers. And she had tiptoed down the hall, refusing even to glance at the door behind which Oliver would be slumbering. But now that door had opened. She turned as he whispered her name once again. "Alexandria, I must talk to you."

She was prepared to stand upon her dignity, to be cool and distant as befitted her new position. But at the sight of him, all her resolution melted. He stood framed in the doorway wearing a pale blue brocade dressing gown fastened to the throat with golden frogs and topped with a velvet collar of darker blue. His hair, usually so carefully arranged, was becomingly sleep-tousled. His chin was covered with the stubble of a beard, so fair as to be almost imperceptible. His handsome face was haggard. His eyes, that matched the blue of his robe so perfectly, were as bloodshot as her own. Alexandria tried to stifle all the old emotions, but it was of no use. Never had Oliver looked so appealing.

"When did you wish to see me?" The words came tumbling out against her will.

"Right away," he whispered. "We may never get another opportunity."

She hesitated just a moment, listening for signs of stirring in Lady Augusta's room, then started for his door.

"Not in here!" Oliver looked alarmed and rather shocked. "Meet me in the morning room in ten minutes' time."

"If I can," she answered, feeling that she'd been rebuffed and trying to sound indifferent.

"Pray do so." The look he gave her was so imploring that all of her resentment died. "I would not impose upon you if I could help myself."

Alexandria used the first few seconds of the time allotted to open Lady Augusta's door a crack and listen to her employer's snoring. If noise was any indication of the depth of slumber, the old lady should not stir for quite some time. Next, Alexandria turned to the looking glass to repair her windblown hair. She took far more care with her appearance than she had done for Harry Romney. She softened her severe hairstyle and allowed some locks to escape their fastening and curl around her face. She noted with satisfaction that the icy cold had brought color to her cheeks and chose to dismiss the fact that her nose was also rosy. After all,

31

one could not hope for everything. Satisfied that she looked at least as presentable as Amelia Fielding, she opened her door slightly, saw that the coast was clear, and headed for the morning room.

Oliver was there before her. He too had used the time on his toilet and had changed his robe for morning dress. But the rumpled state of his usually precise neck cloth and the stubble of his still unshaven chin testified to his haste and the absence of his valet. Again, Alexandria found his unkempt appearance, so alien to his fastidious nature, most appealing.

She had not allowed herself, she thought, to speculate upon why Oliver desired this meeting with her. Perhaps it was simply that she'd come straight from one invitation to run away to Gretna Green and marry that had planted a seed of hope. His first words destroyed it.

"I know I had no right to ask to see you. I promise I shall not do so again."

Her face must have shown the consternation that she felt, for, almost against his will, it seemed, he reached out and took her hand. "And I have no right to care for you still," he continued in a low voice, choked with emotion, "but in spite of everything, I do."

She gazed at him adoringly and would have gone straight into his arms, but he dropped her hand as suddenly as he'd taken it. With a groan he strode away from her to sink down upon a Grecian cross-framed stool and bury his face in his hands. Unbidden, his cousin Harry's description of Oliver's theatrical ability tweaked Alexandria's memory. She pushed the unworthy thought aside as he raised his head to look at her and say, "Forgive me for wasting precious time with my own emotions. I had thought my feelings were well buried, but I was deceived. I promise I will not give way to them again. Nor will I dissemble."

She came across the room and sank down upon the floor beside his stool. Oliver seemed barely able to restrain himself from reaching out to touch her. She moved a little closer in case the impulse struck him once again. But he jumped up and began to stride back and forth in front of her while running his fingers distractedly through his hair.

"As I was saying, I will not dissemble. It is because I still care—still retain feelings for you that more appropriately should be directed elsewhere—that I had to see you."

Alexandria glanced at the door uneasily as she rose from the floor to occupy the vacated stool. She did wish that Oliver would get to the point quickly before someone came to fetch her. He saw the glance and interpreted it correctly.

"Since Lady Augusta may send for you at any moment, forgive me if I am more blunt than I would be if our time were unlimited. I asked for this meeting because I saw you steal out of the house to meet my cousin. And it will not do, Alexandria. It simply will not do."

Her face flamed red. Whatever she had expected, it certainly was not this. "I did not steal out," she retorted hotly, rising to her feet. "Besides, what right have you—"

"None at all," he interrupted. He stopped his pacing to come and stand in front of her. "But I would be remiss in my duty to you as your cousin, not to mention the other ties that once existed between the two of us, if I did not warn you against Henry

Romney. You are far too inexperienced, Alexandria, to have even an inkling of his true character. Suffice it for me to say that, as an unprotected woman, you should keep as far away from him as possible. Such clandestine meetings as I've just witnessed will not do. They would be deemed improper for any gently bred young woman." His finely chiseled lips pursed with disapproval. "But for one in your position—what could you have been thinking of, Alexandria?" What might have begun as a concerned warning suddenly began to sound very much like a scold.

"How dare you spy on me!" Alexandria's voice quivered with indignation.

"I was not spying on you," he retorted. "I simply awoke early and was opening up the curtains when I happened to see Harry go out and enter the maze. Such early activity seemed so out of character on his part," he continued, "that I will confess I was curious and stayed by the window. Frankly, I expected to see one of the housemaids follow him. Such an assignation would be in keeping with his character. You can imagine my shock when I saw *you* emerge and follow him."

"Yes, I can well imagine." Her face had whitened and her eyes blazed at him, but she managed to keep her voice subdued. "Just as I can imagine the much greater shock to anyone who happened by to observe the two of us right now. Why should you assume that my meeting with your cousin was any less innocent?"

"Because I know him. A gently bred young lady such as yourself could not begin to imagine the depths of depravity . . . Well, I shall say no more."

"Indeed you shall say more! You cannot make

such accusations as you've made and then not substantiate them."

His face assumed a pained expression. "I had thought it sufficient merely to point out to you that Henry Romney is not the type of man with whom you should be holding clandestine meetings."

"Well, it is not sufficient. Just what has he done that is so terrible?"

"It would hardly be proper for me to catalog his vices. I do not consider them fit for a lady's ears."

"But you seem to forget that I am no longer a lady. Would you hesitate to tell the parlor maid?"

"Alexandria, stop it! Why must you demean yourself?"

"I did not intend to do so. I was merely trying to explain that in my position I no longer see the point of being missish. And I really do need—want—to know of Harry's reputation."

For a moment she toyed with the notion of telling Oliver the real reason she felt it necessary to explore Henry Romney's character. But she decided to hold her tongue. She knew how much it would upset Oliver to learn that his cousin had made an offer for the young woman he had once planned to wed. She did not wish to wound him, she told herself, though that bothersome inner voice which nagged so much of late suggested that the true reason she did not speak was a lack of faith that Harry would return. She prodded Oliver for further disclosures about his cousin's character.

"I know Harry likes to shock," she said defensively. "But in spite of such affectations as coming to dinner dressed in traveling clothes and blowing a cloud of tobacco in the drawing room, which I would term rude, certainly, but not depraved, I doubt that he is any worse than others of the care-for-nothing set."

"As to that, I could not say. But it's wonderful to me if multiplying vices makes them tolerable. Can you bring yourself to disapprove of him only if he turns out to be the blackest of a very shady lot indeed?"

"I can only bring myself to disapprove of him if you tell me what he has done."

"To say what he has not would be easier."

"Oliver!"

"Very well then, if you insist upon a catalog. Mistresses too numerous to tally. His current light-skirt is an actress to whom he has given a carte blanche. An insignificant actress, I might add. Quite beautiful, so they say, but laughable on stage."

"The less talent, the more sin, then?"

"I beg your pardon?"

"Nothing. I should not have spoken. Pray go on. What else?"

"Brawling of all sorts—fists, pistols, swords. Driving neck-or-nothing through the town. Why, he once took over the ribbons of the Brighton mail, which was filled with passengers, I might add, and raced it against one of his rackety friends who drove a curricle."

"Did he win?" Alexandria asked.

"What does that have to say to anything? It's his morals we are speaking of."

"Well, all that sounds quite childish, but not immoral."

"You might have thought differently if it were your neck in danger of being broken. I can assure you that the passengers were not so charitable as you seem to be."

"No doubt you are right. But I still haven't heard anything that justifies his reputation."

"Just believe me, Alexandria. My cousin is quite at home with all the vices—drink, women, gambling—"

"Gambling?" she quickly interposed.

"Yes, gambling."

Oliver was finally making an impression. Other transgressions in the world of men might be beyond Alexandria's comprehension. But she was all too well acquainted with the evil effects of hazard. He chose to elaborate. "My cousin is a member of Watier's and is said to play as deep as any of their gentlemen." He sneered at the term. "Nor is the wagering there confined to the usual games of chance. The members are like to bet on anything—horses, two flies on the wall, how soon a persistent suitor can break down a female's virtue . . ."

"You need go no further." Alexandria looked fully as disgusted as Oliver could have wished. "I'm well acquainted with the methods used to dissipate fortunes which have been in families for generations."

"Now perhaps you can tell me why you were so concerned to learn the details of my cousin's vices," Oliver said. "Why were you not content just to accept my warning in the same spirit in which I gave it? Has that libertine made love to you? If so, I must warn you that his intentions will always be less than honorable."

"No, of course he has not made love to me," she answered, pleased at Oliver's obvious jealousy. "I merely wished to know why I should snub the only one of my former acquaintances who has treated me the way I was once accustomed to being treated." She had not meant to allow the bitterness to creep into her voice.

"I'm sorry." Oliver's face reflected the pain she felt and he stepped forward, seemingly without thinking, and took her into his arms. "Alexandria, I'm so sorry. So very sorry."

She looked up from where she'd instinctively rested her head upon his shoulder and saw tears brimming in his eyes. "You do still love me. Don't try to hide it," she whispered, raising her mouth to his, giving him no chance to form a quick denial. And his lips, pressing so urgently, so hungrily upon hers, gave the answer that she longed to hear. Alexandria returned Oliver's kiss passionately, with far more ardor than she'd ever allowed herself to show before, her desire born of separation and despair. She pressed her body tightly against his and entwined her fingers in his golden curls as if she would hold on forever and never let him go. It was Oliver who at length pushed himself free and turned away with a tortured groan.

"Oh, my God, what have I done?"

"You've simply come to realize you still love me." Alexandria was flushed and triumphant now, sure of him once again. "Oh, Oliver, I knew you had to come to your senses finally. I knew you could not actually go through with it."

He turned a shocked face toward her. "Not go through with it? Whatever do you mean?"

"I mean Lady Amelia Fielding. Of course you cannot marry her. Knowing, as you've just rediscovered, that you are in love with me."

"I have no choice," he answered miserably. "The wedding is a bare week away. Besides, you should not think—you must not think—just because I lost control for a moment that anything has changed."

"Of course I think it! You cannot marry her." She

reached out to clutch at his sleeve in desperation. "You cannot enter into a loveless marriage. You cannot sacrifice our future happiness merely for the sake of Lady Amelia's fortune. It's—it's—despicable."

"You much mistake the matter," he answered stiffly. "To act in any other way, that would be despicable. To put my own interest above that of my family and its name. You know as well as I that the Linnell estates have been steadily dwindling during the last three generations. If your father had not lost your holdings, things might have been different. Though not nearly so extensive as Lady Amelia's, they would have been sufficient to let me follow my heart without impoverishing the next generations of Linnells. But now there can be no question of my marrying imprudently."

"But others marry for love and are the better for it. You could forget the estates, find employment . . ."

He looked at her, appalled. He could have been no more shocked if she'd suggested murder. "Surely you do not expect me to enter a trade?"

"No, no, of course not," she replied hastily, seeing how deeply offended he was. "It's just—just"—tears brimmed into her eyes—"just that I don't know how I shall contrive ever to live without you."

"Nor I without you," he replied huskily, folding her into his arms again and kissing her more tenderly this time, and more sorrowfully. It was a farewell kiss, she realized; the valedictory of their love. And she yearned to prolong it as long as possible.

A throat cleared loudly behind them. Oliver leaped backward while at the same time giving Alexandria a shove. Half a room's distance lay between them before the false "Har-rumph" had drawn to its conclusion. Alexandria turned her horrified gaze toward the door to see Lady Augusta's ancient maid Clarissa standing there, her face impassive but her eyes fairly snapping with excitement.

"Her ladyship is inquiring for you, miss," she said.

Chapter Four

"COME IN, COME IN, ALEXANDRIA. GOOD OF YOU TO fit me into your busy schedule." Lady Augusta's voice was heavily sarcastic. Nor was her glare encouraging. She was sitting propped up in bed by pillows, her nightcap askew, with wisps of thin grey hair dangling out from under it. She was clearly out of sorts, an attitude not unusual with the dowager.

Alexandria chose to blame the port for her employer's mood. She did not doubt that Lady Augusta had found her way to the clothes press more than once after her companion had gone to bed. Now she likely had the headache. That could account for her grouchiness. After all, Alexandria had only paused to tidy her loosened hair before reporting to Lady Augusta's bedchamber. That hardly gave Clarissa time ...

"It won't do, you know." Her ladyship's glare of disapproval grew, cutting short Alexandria's optimistic musings. "I won't have you throwing yourself at Oliver's head like some lovesick parlor maid. It will not do!"

"I did not throw myself at Oliver's head." Alexandria closed the door behind her, certain that her employer's carrying voice had already drifted down the hall.

"Liar!" Lady Augusta barked. "Come over here where I can see you."

Alexandria walked obediently toward the bed, recalling Harry's words about locking up the knives and hiding the blunt instruments.

"What do you have to say for yourself?"

"What may I do for you? Shall I fetch you the newspaper and read it?"

"Hoity-toity! So that's your ploy, is it? Think to fob me off and change the subject. Well, it won't do. Sit down, girl. I'll not make my headache worse by stiffening my neck looking up at you." When Alexandria had obediently drawn up a chair she continued. "How dare you deny that you were kissing Oliver? Clarissa has been with me these sixty years now and if she says she saw a thing, she saw it."

"I did not deny I was kissing Oliver." Alexandria's voice retained its dignity, though her cheeks were flaming hot. "What I denied was throwing myself at him. I can assure, he was the instigator."

"Was he now?" The old lady suddenly lost her forbidding aspect and began to chuckle. "Well, he's more warm-blooded than I gave him credit for. Oh, wouldn't I have given a monkey if it had been that screeching Amelia Fielding who caught you instead of Clarissa. That would have been a rare dust-up, sure enough." She sighed regretfully, then immediately cheered up. "Of course, she's bound to hear of it soon enough. The servants know everything that goes on here—you'd best keep that in mind—and none of my staff can abide that uppity French maid the Fieldings brought. They'll fall all over themselves giving her the news, you mark my words." She chuckled delightedly at the thought, then glared once more. "But I don't mind saying that I ain't pleased at having my companion the *on-dit* of the servants' hall. Your conduct this morning is not becoming to your position."

"Well," Alexandria said wearily, "I won't deny that you are right. But do not distress yourself. You must also be aware that it's not likely to be repeated."

"True," her employer replied. "And I still say I'm surprised that it happened once. Oh, I know that you'd be willing enough." She closed Alexandria's protesting mouth with a wave of her hand. "Don't bother denying it. I've seen you look at Oliver. But what surprises me is that he'd risk having his fiancée get into a taking over you and break off the engagement. Not that I think for a minute she would. She's as daft over him as you are. But the fact remains, Oliver's not sure of that, and he's not one to let his feelings rule his head. So I wouldn't have expected him to be making love to you.

"Fond of the boy, of course," she went on, "but I've always thought him rather a cold fish. Not like that hot-spur Harry. Well, it certainly says something for you. Oliver losing his head, I mean." She looked Alexandria up and down as if seeing her for the first time. "Humph! You're a good-looking enough chit, I suppose. Though you can't compare to the women in my day. Now we were real beauties, with our patches and pompadours—but enough of that. It still says something in your favor when you can make Oliver lose his head. But you'd best not refine too much on it. Oliver's too prudent to marry you and too prudish to offer you carte blanche."

"Really, Lady Augusta! I think this conversation has gotten—"

Alexandria might as well not have spoken, for her employer was pursuing a new thought. "Harry might, though. Now, there's an idea for you. I understand you met him in the maze before making love to Oliver." She chuckled. "And you so proper and proud that butter wouldn't even melt in your mouth. Still waters certainly do run deep. But, as I was saying, you just might be able to get a carte blanche out of Harry." She waved her hand imperiously to stop Alexandria's protest. "I know what you're going to say. He already has one Cyprian tucked away in a love nest somewhere. But, la! I doubt that would stop Harry Romney. He ain't the faithful sort. And lord knows he can afford to set up any number of females in style if he's a mind to."

"If you think for one moment that I'd—" Alexandria was on the verge of apoplexy.

"No, I don't suppose you would. The more fool you." The old lady shook her head. "And when it comes down to it, I doubt that even Harry would dare offer it. A pity that. The problem is, you really are beyond the pale where gentlemen are concerned. Too poor for marrying and too well bred for keeping. Well, perhaps a suitable curate will come along. Or some well-to-do cit who owns one of those filthy factories that keep springing up everywhere may want to raise his station in life by marrying into a good family. It ain't likely, though, for I'd never let such inside my doors. No, missy, no matter how many scalawags you may have kissed this morning, I expect you're stuck with me. So go fetch that paper you were asking to read me and let's see what mischief Prinny's up to now. And tell Clarissa to hurry with my tea."

By the time Alexandria had read the choicest tidbits of news to her employer, mostly having to do with Napoleon's stubborn refusal to know when he was beaten, but with considerable space devoted to the usual veiled allusions to the old King's madness and the not-so-veiled criticisms of the Regent's extravagances, and by the time she had listened to Lady Augusta's pithy comments made between loud sips of tea, it was well past ten o'clock.

Alexandria had hoped that the remnants of the breakfast spread would still be on the sideboard but that the guests would be fed and gone. It almost worked that way. Unfortunately, the two Fielding sisters were still eating.

Lady Amelia and Lady Arabel gave Alexandria the coolest of nods as she entered the breakfast parlor. Any hope that Oliver's fiancée was unaware of their morning tryst died instantly. Bonaparte could use the spy network in this house to his advantage, Alexandria thought bitterly, pouring out her tea. Nothing she did seemed to go unnoticed. When there was time to think of it, she promised herself, she would try to unravel the mystery of how Lady Augusta had learned of her early-morning adventure in the maze.

Regretting that she'd come to breakfast, Alexandria took only a roll and butter with her tea and settled herself as far from the Fieldings as possible. The sisters ignored her completely, continuing their low-voiced conversation, which obviously was not intended for her ears, but which she could hardly avoid overhearing.

". . . left for London without even telling Lady Augusta of his intent," Lady Arabel was whispering, her fat curls shaking with indignation. It was apparent why the two were still at table well after the other guests had gone. Lady Arabel's plate was piled high with broken eggshells and cold pork bones. She was now sipping chocolate and devouring rich plum cake. "And no one even seems surprised at such rackety behavior," she added.

"Indeed, it is not wonderful to me," her sister sniffed. "He is a noted care-for-nothing. Totally wanting in civility, and a cruel jokester too. They say that when he broke off with one of his mistresses she wrote him a note asking for the return of her lock of hair. What did he do but send his valet to her house with at least a dozen locks of every color and a request that, since he had difficulty recalling just which it was, she pick out her own."

Alexandria choked on her tea, but her strangling went unnoticed. The sisters broke off their conversation as another tardy breakfast guest arrived.

Oliver had already taken several steps into the room before noticing the three of them. He stopped dead in his tracks and turned red, much to Alexandria's chagrin and his fiancée's annoyance.

That lady recovered first. She bent her haughty, impersonal gaze upon Alexandria. "Miss Linnell, would you please fetch my needlework for me? I would ring for one of the maids but they are quite overworked with all the extra guests. In contrast, your own duties seem to leave you ample freedom."

Lady Arabel gave a high-pitched giggle at her sister's last remark. Otherwise the room was deathly silent.

Alexandria noted, as one might watch an actor in a play, that Oliver's cheeks had gone from red to chalky white and that his hands were clenched tightly into fists. It was, finally, her fear that Oliver would take his bride-to-be to task for treating his cousin like a servant—or perhaps the sudden, craven fear that he would not—that made Alexandria bite back the retort her tongue was forming and rise meekly to her feet.

"Yes, of course," she answered calmly, noting that Lady Amelia lowered her eyes before her steady gaze. "Will I find it in your bedchamber?"

"Yes. In the work table by the window. And you need not bother to return it here. My sister and I shall repair to the morning room."

Alexandria made her way to Lady Amelia's room more from memory than by sight, for she walked through a red haze of blinding anger. She snatched up the landscape picture in colored silk—a drab thing, like its creator, she noted spitefully—and ran with it to the morning room, colliding with a startled upstairs maid in the process. Ignoring the work table strategically placed to catch the morning light, she flung the embroidery upon the sofa in the farfetched hope that, before discovering its presence there, Lady Amelia's ample posterior might come into contact with the needle. The absurdity of such a petty notion of revenge lowered her spirits even further. "Dogsbody!" she muttered softly to herself. "Fetch my shawl! Fetch my needlework! Go to the devil!"

Perhaps it was the unaccustomed oath that put her in mind of Harry Romney and gave her the courage to put on her cloak and pattens for the second time that morning and go outside. "Let them ring the house down," she muttered between clenched teeth. "I've had enough."

The feeble sun could be perceived only in dim outline and the gusting wind was every bit as raw as it had been earlier. But this time she welcomed the icy blasts that stung her cheeks and filled her eyes with justifiable tears. "Harry will do well to make it to London before it snows," she thought with a country woman's bent for weather prophesying. It was not his getting to London, however, that concerned her. The burning question was, would he ever come back?

The morning's events had moved far too fast for thought. Already the strange proposal in the maze seemed like a dream. She'd had such dreams before. Caught in some terrible predicament from which there could be no escape, suddenly, impossibly, she'd see an escape avenue open up, clear and inviting.

Well, Harry Romney's was no honorable, clear invitation. Indeed, if she listened to Oliver it was quite the contrary. "Go to the devil." Alexandria whispered the words to herself once more and vowed to take her own advice. Oh, don't be so dramatic, her less emotional nature chided. That's coming it a bit strong. She doubted that Harry was quite as villainous as Oliver had painted him. Oliver Linnell was no unbiased judge of his cousin's character. In fact, Alexandria reflected, the two had

48

been most uncousinly from their cradle days—one more proof, perhaps, of Harry's illegitimacy.

No, Oliver was not the best judge of Harry's character. But even if he were, she stoutly told herself, she did not care. Harry could frequent every whorehouse, rat pit, boxing ring, gambling hell—

She broke off her vice list with a shudder. There was the rub, and well she knew it. She could overlook almost any transgression on Harry's part but that one. For she believed him when he'd said they'd lead their lives apart. None of his other vices had to touch her. Whispers and gossip she could live with; they would be a small enough price to pay for the return of her dignity and her pride. But gambling was an obsession that reached out to destroy the lives of everyone connected with the gamester. Even without her father's grim example and the consequent ruin of her life, there were countless other tales of family fortunes wiped out by one evening's disastrous gaming. And Watier's, that exclusive club for gentlemen that boasted Henry Romney among its members, was notorious for deep play.

Alexandria sighed and admitted to herself that gambling must be also in her blood. For she knew that, in spite of all her fears, she would not hesitate to stake her life on this turn of fortune's wheel that Harry offered.

Alexandria knew she had no choice. She might fume and rail over Lady Augusta's insulting arrogance. She might consider Lady Amelia's bit of "run and fetch" to be the final straw. But all that was simply subterfuge—an attempt to cloud the issue. The real hurt was this: Oliver, who said he loved her, still planned to marry someone else. Well, two could play that game. She would run, not walk, to Harry Romney.

The question was, would Harry come to her?

Chapter Five

ALEXANDRIA HAD TURNED BACK IN DESPAIR TOWARD her employer's manor house and was, indeed, some twenty yards up the carriage drive before the sound of wheels sent her running hopefully back toward the gate. Shading her eyes against the sun just peeping over the horizon, she felt the prick of tears, whether from the glare or from the disappointment she could not say. The rays prevented her seeing more than an outline of the approaching vehicle, but it was enough to see it couldn't be Harry's. "I should have known he wouldn't come. Damn Harry Romney anyhow," she muttered as she turned away, using the profanity as a substitute for weeping. After having waited for ages in the cold and darkness, Alexandria found this final disappointment too much to bear. She hurried toward the house, anxious to regain her lost composure before having to face Lady Augusta and the rest of her shattered life.

She didn't trouble to turn around as she heard the driver coax his speeding horses to a halt. If he wanted to ask directions, let him look for someone else.

"Alex!"

The whoop stopped her in her tracks.

"Alex, where the devil are you off to? Come on, get in! We're late enough already as it is."

"Well, whose fault is that?" Relief turned her waspish as she wheeled to see that it was, indeed, Harry Romney there, holding his matched greys in check, much against their wills.

"Mine, I suppose," he retorted, tugging skillfully at the reins. "Though why you decided to turn tail at the sight of me I couldn't hope to fathom."

Alexandria had hastily closed the gap between them and was now staring up at the driver in disbelief. If her look was incredulous, his was jaundiced. The Honorable Henry Romney was decidedly the worse for wear—unshaven and bleary-eyed, with a crease between his eyebrows that signaled the pressure of a headache. He wore the same curly-brimmed beaver at the same jaunty angle as when he'd proposed his marriage scheme. And the caped greatcoat was as elegant as before, but the shirt points and neck cloth revealed by its open buttons seemed far too long removed from the ministrations of a trained manservant. Harry's temper seemed prepared to go out of control along with the folds of his cravat. Alexandria took in the warning signs, but failed to heed them.

"I turned tail, as you call it," she spat at him, "because I did not think this could possibly be you."

"No?" he said sarcastically, reaching a hand down to help her up. She ignored the hand, and he frowned. "Who else would be calling for you at this hellish hour? Just how many elopements have you scheduled? Why the devil didn't you think it was me?"

"Because I never dreamed you'd be driving that!" She waved her hand disparagingly at what really was the latest crack, a two-wheeled curricle of gleaming black with cream-colored leather upholstery and trim.

Mr. Romney took exception to her tone. *"That,"* he echoed. "What the devil do you mean by *that*? I'll have you know that this is probably the finest, best-sprung rig to be found. And since when are you any judge of—"

"I've no intention of insulting your rig," she intervened. "It's no doubt greatly admired in Hyde Park. It just seems an odd choice for several days of travel. I'm surprised you did not bring a hobbyhorse," she added, referring to the two-wheeled, foot-propelled vehicles which had become the craze. "It would have been every bit as practical."

"Practical! What could be more practical than a curricle?" Mr. Romney sputtered.

"A hay cart, a balloon basket—anything which is not totally exposed to the elements on a winter journey to Scotland. And something with room enough for both of us, not to mention—"

"There's plenty of room—unless you've spread more than the younger Lady Fielding since I last saw you."

"Not to mention hot bricks and luggage." She stopped aghast. "Luggage! You said I need not bring anything, that you'd take care of it. You said—"

"Alex!" Mr. Romney looked downright dangerous. "Do you or do you not wish to go to Scotland and marry me?"

"Y-yes."

"Then, I'm sorry I did not provide a coach and four. But I did not wish to bring along an entourage either. In fact, what I mostly wished to do was to get to my destination as quickly as possible. I would suggest that, if you're unhappy with the accommodations, you can take the public coach. But I'm afraid that won't serve either, for I've no intention of cooling my heels in Gretna Green waiting for you to arrive. Also, I've no intention of holding these horses any longer. Either climb up here and let's be off or go back and resume fetching Aunt Augusta's false teeth, or whatever it is you spend your time doing there. Ordinarily I enjoy a good discussion as well as the next fellow, but not when I have the headache and not before breakfast—please. Facts you might try to keep in mind if you intend to wed me. Well, do you?"

"Yes, of course," Alexandria answered crossly, clambering into the curricle with the minimum of assistance from her fiancé. "That is, I will marry you if I don't die of the grippe between here and Scotland."

"Small chance. You don't look the delicate type to me," Harry Romney said ungallantly, cracking his whip and springing his horses. "Besides, your flaming temper should keep you hot enough, even without a brick for your dainty feet."

Alexandria was too busy keeping her balance on the seat as Harry's team tore down the road to reply to his last sally. But when the pace finally slowed a bit, she stole a look at his scowling face and cleared her throat tentatively. "I'm sorry," she said in a quite small voice.

He took his eyes off the team and the road to pierce her with a bloodshot stare. "Sorry? What the devil are you sorry for?"

"For railing at you as I did. I had absolutely no right to. For really I'm most grateful. The truth is, I'd quite despaired of your coming, and I was sure I was doomed to spend my life fetching Lady Augusta's teeth. And I think the reason I was so shrewish was because I was so terribly disappointed when I thought it wasn't you. You see, I had rather expected a closed carriage. But a curricle is actually a splendid idea. The air is quite bracing, and the point you made about speed is certainly well taken." She gasped as they took a curve on the inside wheel and clutched at one of his capes in order to hang on. "As I was saying," she continued as soon as the team hit a straightaway, "I should not have lost my temper in that odious way, and I do beg—"

"Alex!" Mr. Romney's thundering voice interrupted her apology and spurred his startled team on even faster. "Do, for God's sake, be quiet. Can't you hear yourself? One more minute and you'll actually be groveling." He turned his haughty stare on her again.

"I was merely trying to be civil," she retorted, bewildered by his anger but feeling her own temper rising to match it.

"The devil take your civility," he snapped back. "You were acting like a hired companion. In your mind you've just traded old Augusta for me, am I not right?"

She was about to hurl a denial but the justice of his accusation hit her. "I suppose so," she answered uncomfortably. "After all, it's very much the same."

"That's where you're wrong. I'm not Aunt Augusta, damn it, to be coaxed and cossetted out of an ill humor. And you are to be my wife, not someone who cannot express an opinion for fear of being turned off without a character. You are shortly to become a Romney, so for God's sake start acting like one."

"Oh, and how exactly is that done?" Alexandria's voice dripped heavy sarcasm. "Which shall I work on first, arrogance or rudeness?"

"Whichever you wish. Just as long as you abandon toad-eating altogether."

"Toad-eating! I was not toad-eating. I was merely trying to behave like a person of breeding. Which won't do for a Romney, come to think on it. But civility is a hard habit for me to break. For, after all, I am a Linnell. And I might point out that my family was distinguishing itself in court circles while the Romneys were, no doubt, still painting their faces blue."

The Honorable Henry Romney let go the reins a moment to clap his hands in polite applause. "Well, thank God." He grinned at her suddenly as he picked up the ribbons again. "I was afraid that between them old Augusta and Oliver had done you irreparable harm. But I can see that underneath all that sniveling servility there still beats the heart of that little termagant who went for me with the stick."

"I cannot see why that incident should have stayed in your mind for all these years," she replied crossly. "I can imagine that most people who are in your company for long are driven to some sort of violence."

"Only the courageous," he answered flippantly. "You'd be surprised at the number of people who choose to fawn on me instead."

"I certainly wasn't fawning. And when you accused me of toad-eating, you forgot one thing."

"Indeed? And what was that?"

"That we struck a bargain. In return for your emancipating me, I was not to interfere with you. That's what you said. I was merely trying to keep my end of the agreement."

"That's not the same thing at all." He slowed the team a bit as they approached a crossroads. "You can live and let live without winding up a doormat."

"I don't see how. If I showed my anger over the fact that you kept me waiting for simply ages, and then when you finally did show up you were driving an open curricle and were without any of the luggage that you promised me, and if I demanded an explanation, that's interfering with your life. Am I not right?"

"No. I would not say so. If you wish an explanation, you only have to ask."

"Very well, then, since you give me leave. Why were you late and in a curricle and unshaved and looking a perfect mess and without the things you promised to furnish me?"

"Because I was playing cards and could not break up the game early. And in order to get here at all I had to leave from Watier's just as I was. Satisfied?"

"Not really," she answered stiffly. "But if I were

57

to express my true opinion of your conduct, you would have grounds for complaint, am I not right?"

"You mean if you should take it upon yourself to lecture me upon the evils of gambling? I'd call it a dead bore, of that you can be sure, at least."

"I can see that my position is going to be quite complicated," she retorted, lapsing into silence. Then, for the first time, she allowed her attention to turn from her companion to the countryside. She stared at the inn which they were rapidly approaching. "That almost looks like—" she remarked. "But it can't be. But it is! That's the Golden Cock!" She grabbed the Honorable Henry's arm, causing the horses to swerve suddenly while the driver swore. "For heaven's sake, do you realize you are going in the wrong direction entirely? This really is the outside of enough! You'll have to turn around there in the inn yard. Scotland is that way." She wheeled in her seat to point dramatically.

"No, you are quite mistaken." But he slowed down his horses nonetheless.

"I am not mistaken. I have been in this area far too long not to know directions. This is the way to London."

"True," he answered, "but that was not my point of contradiction. It was Scotland's location that was in question and I merely wished to mention that you were gesturing so theatrically toward the Isle of Man."

"That's as may be and has nothing to say to anything anyhow. The point is, you are taking me in quite the wrong direction entirely and now you say it is not even by accident." She looked at him with bitterness. "Oliver and Lady Augusta were right about you. They said you would never marry me.

That it was more in your style to offer a carte blanche."

Mr. Romney took a moment to reply. He skillfully weaved his team into the bustling yard of the Golden Cock, maneuvering between a private carriage that had stopped for a change of horses and the stage coach for Carlisle, which was trying to shift the passengers on top to accommodate a stout gentleman with a large wicker basket which from the sound of it, contained a goose. But after Mr. Romney had pulled his greys to a halt near the entrance of the inn, he turned his full attention back to Alexandria, looking down his crooked nose in a way that made her most uncomfortable, as if she saw her shabby drabness reflected in his eyes.

"Cousin Oliver and Aunt Augusta predicted that I'd offer you carte blanche, did they? Well, they could not be more wrong. Frankly, Alex, I would not offer you sixpence for that type of accommodation, let alone open my purse strings entirely. Now, if you're through jumping to conclusions, you might jump down and bespeak our breakfast while I go to hire that coach you wanted."

Alexandria judged that her face had now flamed red enough to match her frozen nose from the setdown he'd delivered. "You need not hire a coach for me," she said with what dignity she could muster. "I have quite resigned myself to the curricle. It's—it's—most exhilarating."

"It's a bit late for that after, as you so dramatically pointed out, we've gone out of our way to get here. Besides," he added, helping her none too gently to the ground, "you are not the sole person concerned, if you'll pardon my saying so." With

59

that, he strode off toward the stables, leaving her to enter the inn alone.

Nor did his temper improve when he came into the travellers' waiting room a few minutes later to find her seated at a large table near the fire with two seedy-looking males and an elderly farm couple. "Did you not ask for a private parlor?" he demanded, impervious to the resentful stares of his fellow guests.

"You did not tell me to."

"I never dreamed that it would be necessary. Landlord!" he roared.

That worthy, recognizing the voice of authority when he heard it, appeared at once, bowing obsequiously. His bow was arrested in midarc, however, when he took full note of the caller. There was no denying the superior cut of the tall young man's tailoring, but his unkempt appearance, aided by a rather dangerous expression, was forcing the landlord to change his category from gentleman to highwayman, or worse.

Harry, taking full note of his host's equivocation, pulled forth a roll of bank notes from the recesses of his greatcoat. "A private parlor for the lady and myself," he barked, peeling off a bill of sufficient denomination to cause the landlord to lose all qualms. "And add some ham and eggs and ale to whatever it was you'd intended to foist off upon the lady. And, oh yes," he added, as the landlord hastily ushered them into a small room next to the larger one, while a servant scurried after them to light the fire that was already laid there in the fireplace, "do you have a wife on the premises? Or some other female with a bit of judgment?"

"My wife is here, sir." The corpulent landlord's

eyes bugged at this new sign of his eccentric guest's oddity.

"Then please ask her to come here at once," Harry commanded, walking up to the fireplace, where the servant was using his lungs for an ineffective bellows. He gave the back log a well-placed kick that later made his valet wince at the damage done to the surface of his Hessian boot, so lovingly kept gleaming with boot-blacking and champagne. He succeeded, however, in sending the sparks flying up the chimney, and was standing with his back to a crackling blaze when the landlady entered the room a few moments later.

A large, shrewd-looking woman, she was not so easily flustered as her husband. She took one look at Alexandria, seemed assured of her respectability, urged her to move her chair closer to the fire, and informed her that hot tea was on its way. "Which will warm you from the inside out in no time," she said. Having done the important things, she then turned her attention to the cut-throat young man, who was glaring impatiently. "You wished to see me, sir?"

"Yes, I did. Would you please stand up, Alex?" Alexandria opened her mouth—to question or protest—then did just as he had asked.

"We're on our way to Gretna Green," Harry informed the landlord's wife. "Unfortunately, we had to leave in something of a rush, and the lady had no time to provide herself with the necessities. Do you think you might—in an hour's time at the outside—find suitable clothing to tide her over for a trip to Scotland and back to London? You know— night clothes, a hair brush, I suppose . . ." He looked at Alexandria inquiringly and she nodded in

61

embarrassment. "In short, whatever females need to keep them going. Do you think you can manage?" He peeled off an amount of currency that made Alexandria's eyes bulge but left the other woman unimpressed.

"Possibly. We'll see, won't we? Well, now, here's your breakfast, my dear." The landlady obviously was feeling protective toward Alexandria. Her speculative glance at the Honorable Henry left no doubt that she suspected that this was no romantic elopement but an abduction, perhaps at gunpoint.

Alexandria tried to reassure the woman by thanking her in advance for all her trouble.

"Don't thank me yet," the good lady retorted, with another black glance at Harry. "In spite of what some folk think, I'm not Rumpelstiltskin, to be weaving up clothes miraculously. But I do have an idea or two in my head. We'll see what comes of it."

She bustled out of the room while her underlings began to lay out the breakfast spread on a table before the fire. As they did so, the Honorable Henry, wandering impatiently about the room, caught a glimpse of himself in a mirror placed over a small side table.

He stroked his heavy bristle ruefully. "I say there," he called to a retreating waiter, "could you find someone to shave me? No, never mind. Just get me a razor and some hot water and I'll do the job myself. Only give me time to eat first. Come on, Alex."

He drew out her chair and surveyed the spread before them, his satisfaction mingled with surprise. "By Jove, I do believe they've done fairly well by us." He sat down opposite her and bade her pour the tea. "Well, now then. I think that's taken care of everything." His voice was smug with satisfaction. "Let's refuel ourselves. Then it's on to Gretna Green."

Chapter
Six

ALEXANDRIA POSTPONED THINKING OF THE FACT that this was her wedding night. Instead, she first tried counting strokes as she brushed her hair before the dressing-table glass in the inn where they were staying, but it did not serve. So she then reflected, with slightly more success, upon the power of money.

Money, or the lack of it, had always loomed large in her family's life. Even before her father had played his last disastrous card game, it had been in short supply, with their creditors forever beating figuratively—and literally, more than once—upon the door. When Alexandria had undertaken to make her own way in the world, she had had even more reason to despair over the elusiveness of money. And so during the past few hours her eyes had fairly bugged from watching

Harry spread around so much of what he termed his blunt.

First there had been the matter of the Golden Cock. Not only had his wealth produced an actual trousseau—for the resourceful landlady had bought part of the bridal clothes being prepared by the local seamstress for the squire's daughter—it had even produced clean linen for Harry from the landlord's supply.

"It may be on the largish side, since John does like his mutton, as you can see by the belly room allowed." The landlord's wife had waved the enormous shirt as if she planned to use it to make up the bed. "And even if it fit, it's obviously not what you're accustomed to. But it does have the virtue of being clean. And if you can't appreciate that the young lady surely will." Harry had thereupon accepted the landlady's offering with a grace that did little to elevate him in her eyes.

His wealth had also produced a very well sprung coach indeed, along with a spirited team and a coachman to drive them first to Gretna Green, then all the way to London.

"Do you always carry so much money?" she'd inquired as they left the Golden Cock to resume their journey.

"Of course not," he'd replied carelessly. "No use inviting some cove to try and knock you on the head for it. This roll was the bank at Watier's, which took me a bit longer than I'd counted on to win, and kept you waiting for me so patiently. Though, considering I started a day late, I believe I made it in record time. Good thing, actually, that we were playing deep since I didn't dare go back home for anything. Didn't want to distress you by being really late. If you got into such a taking over just an hour, God knows what a day or so would have done. Of course, I could have simply marched up to Aunt Augusta's door and pulled you out, but I like to avoid that kind of dust-up when I can."

"You mean you just got up from the gaming table and climbed in your curricle and came up here without a stop? That's beyond belief!"

"Of course I stopped. Had to change horses, you know."

"But you didn't sleep?"

"I managed a wink or two while they changed cattle."

"Just how would you have managed," she said with heavy sarcasm, "had you been the loser and not the winner in the game?"

"I'm never the loser," he'd replied and, ignoring her derisive snort, he'd made himself as comfortable as possible on the carriage seat and had gone instantly to sleep.

He'd slept through the entire day and journey, only rousing himself as they entered the Scottish marriage capital.

Again he'd demonstrated the power of wealth by quickly persuading a reluctant clergyman to desert his supper, collect a second witness—the grinning coachman having been already paid to serve—and perform the marriage ceremony. Then, before Alexandria had time to realize that she was now legally Mrs. Romney, he had hurried her back into the coach and on to this inn on the London highway.

There Harry's ill-gotten gains had provided the best accommodations in the house, and they had dined sumptuously upon stuffed broiled haddock with suet dumplings, roasted leg of lamb, Jerusalem artichokes, and, for a sweet, gooseberry pudding. He had ordered up hot baths. She had had hers already. He was now splashing noisily in the adjoining dressing room.

For just a moment, as his cheerful whistling penetrated her consciousness, Alexandria did allow herself to recollect that this was her wedding night.

As a young girl she had dreamed the usual romantic dreams about marriage. And the dreams had always cast Oliver in the bridegroom's role. So it was only natural now to pretend once more, to imagine it was really Oliver next door, splashing in the hip bath, whistling gaily, while he readied himself to come to her. She could picture him emerging in his long nightshirt and robe, his fair hair curling damply around his head. She could see his shy smile as he saw her waiting for him in bed, her hair fanned out upon the pillow. She saw his blue eyes light with longing as he moved quickly toward her, tossing his brocade dressing gown upon the floor, removing his nightshirt to pause a moment in his male nakedness, looking for all the world like a marble god come to life as she stretched her welcoming arms out toward him.

"Damn it all!" The whistling came to an abrupt stop and Oliver's image disappeared as the Honorable Henry Romney evidently dropped his soap.

Alexandria sighed for what could never be, pushed away the thought of Oliver, husband to Lady Amelia now, and brushed her hair a little harder.

Then for just a moment she allowed herself to think what it would be like if Harry were the one. She shivered involuntarily. Although Oliver had never allowed himself many liberties even when it was understood they would wed some day, Alexandria was not ignorant of the physical side of marriage. And she knew Oliver well enough to have expected him to be all gentle tenderness on their wedding night. But Harry, her instincts told her, might be quite another matter. Well, he had promised to leave her alone. Besides, he'd made it more than clear that he did not desire her.

She leaned closer to the glass and scanned her appearance. Even the dim candlelight could not obscure the fact that the squire's daughter's gown was designed to be seductive. It was a trifle large for Alexandria, which meant that it exposed even more bosom than had been intended. For no reason at all, Alexandria found herself wondering what Harry's mistress looked like. There really was not that much wrong with her, she thought defensively, recalling his set-down at her mention of carte blanche.

She was standing now before the looking glass, turning her body this way and that as the soft material clung revealingly. "I certainly look like a real bride—too much so, in fact," she muttered as she leaned forward for a closer look and bared her nipples. At that moment she heard a final splash as Harry left the tub. She sprang for her pelisse.

"Are you cold?" Harry looked at her in some surprise, then at the fire roaring up the chimney.

The only resemblance between the Honorable Henry and the ideal bridegroom Alexandria had conjured up was that his hair was indeed dampened from his bath. But instead of curling in a blond halo, it had darkly resisted his rather amateurish efforts to brush it into a stylish Brutus and still trod its own straight path. He wore no brocade robe either, but was dressed in the Golden Cock landlord's outsized shirt, which could easily have accommodated two of him. And he held his scuffed-up Hessians in his hand while he looked at Alexandria uneasily.

"Don't tell me you really have come down with a chill from riding in that curricle. I would have thought you were healthy as a horse. Move closer to the fire and I'll fetch someone. Perhaps if you had a glass—"

Alexandria's expression must have somehow betrayed her, for suddenly Harry's anxious look was replaced with a broad grin. "Well, I'm damned. Here I was worried that you'd contracted a case of grippe and actually you've simply come down with a case of modesty. What do you have on under that depressing garment?"

"I don't know what you mean," she said. "There's nothing odd about feeling chilly."

"Fustian. This fire could burn down London. No wonder your cheeks are red. And here I thought it was from fever. The squire's daughter must have a rare taste in nightdresses. A pity her own poor bridegroom will never see it. Pity about this bridegroom too, come to think of it. You've piqued my curiosity. I don't suppose . . . ?"

"Most certainly not!"

"I was afraid of that." He sat down and began pulling on his boots, then looked at them with a sigh. "I don't know which will undo my valet more, these boots or this tentish shirt. In any case, it may mean the parting of our ways. His brother worked for Brummel. He's never reconciled himself to putting up with me. I think the sight of me now will unman him entirely." He shrugged himself into his coat—one of Weston's finest creations—and noted the bulges the excess of shirt made in its perfect fit. He sighed again. "I could, I suppose, take a page out of your book and wear my greatcoat. But, no, I'm not quite so willing as you to suffer. I'll go as I am and pray I don't see anyone I know till I'm back to Thomas's ministrations."

"Where are you going? It's ten o'clock." Alexandria blurted it out before she thought, then could have bit her tongue. "I beg your pardon. That's none of my concern."

"You do sound most wifely, considering it's only been—what?—five hours since the ceremony, if you can call it that. But, to answer your question, I'm simply going down to see if there's any activity in this inn. Perhaps, if I'm lucky, a coach will stop for a change of horses. That could put some real excitement into the evening. Of course, if you intend to take off that pelisse, I could stay here. Oh, well, then, I'll be off. Since I slept all day, there's little likelihood of my sleeping tonight—especially on that contraption." He gestured toward the couch. "Is there anything I should do before I go? Poke up the fire, for instance?" He grinned as she gave him a quelling look. "No? Good night, then. I'll try not to disturb you when I come back. Pleasant dreams."

Alexandria should have been quite tired. She'd hardly slept at all the night before, between worrying whether Harry would keep to his plan for the elopement and wondering if she'd have the courage to go with him if he did. And it had been a long and tiring day. Even so, she could not sleep. After extinguishing the candle, she lay wide-eyed, watching the reflection of the fire dance upon the ceiling, willing her eyes to close while they perversely became more and more owl-like with each passing moment. Finally she resigned herself to a night of wakefulness, and, deciding there must be a better way to spend it than watching ceiling shadows, she struck a light, donned her pelisse, picked up her japanned candlestick from the nightstand, and sallied forth to check the travellers' waiting room for anything left there that she might read.

She had heard the clock strike twelve a bit before. The boots set out in front of various doors along the hall testified to the fact that whatever travellers the inn might boast had gone to bed. She made her way carefully down the corridor, shielding the candle with her hand to keep the drafts from extinguishing its little light.

The house was depressing in its silence. There was no cheery murmur of voices anywhere to testify to a convivial gathering in any of the rooms. Nor had there been any outside noises for quite some time. If Harry had hoped for a late-night carriage to liven up the place, he was doomed to disappointment. Even though the moon was full enough to make an evening journey possible, it would seem that no travellers were abroad. This impression was confirmed as she entered the deserted common room.

She gave the room a quick survey, hoping that someone had left at least a newspaper behind. But the only reading matter she spotted was a volume of sermons tucked down among the cushions of a wing chair near the fireplace, on purpose, she concluded, as she held it near the feeble firelight and perused one dry page.

A throat clearing made her jump. She turned to

71

see the boots standing behind her with a bucket full of coal.

"I couldn't sleep and was hoping to find something to read." Alexandria didn't know why she felt she owed an explanation as she stepped aside to let the servant refuel the dying fire.

He was very little past his boyhood. A shock of bright red hair contrasted with a face smudged dark with the blacking of his trade. He threw some coals upon the fire, then ran his fist across his nose, adding more soot to it, while he looked at Alexandria with curiosity.

"Ain't you the bride?"

To her exasperation, Alexandria blushed. "I have just recently married," she admitted.

"At five o'clock it was," the boots said helpfully. How he came to be so well informed was beyond imagining. "If you're looking for your husband"—he prodded the coals until they blazed—"he's gone with Mr. Roker to Mr. Roker's parlor."

"I was not looking for my husband but for a book. Do you know where I might find one?"

"Well, if the landlord or his old lady ever reads anything but the bills, I never caught 'em at it." The boots thoughtfully scratched his head, dimming its glow with coal dust. "I'd ask 'em except they've gone to bed. So's everybody else in the place excepting for you and your husband and of course Mr. Roker. But then his is mostly a nighttime trade. And I'm up, too," he added glumly, "till all the boots is finished, which they can't be till everybody else is gone to bed." He stared fixedly at Alexandria, and she watched with fascination the process of an idea turning his expression from downcast all the way to hopeful. "Course if you was to fetch your gentleman out of Mr. Roker's room, we could all turn in."

"I could hardly do that." She had meant to be dismissive, but the boots was loath to let go of the idea.

"Well, it would be a good job of work all round if you was to," he said. "I'd get me sleep, and in the end your old man would thank you for it, for he'll be a lot plumper in the pocket tomorrow if you put an end to his activities right now."

He had Alexandria's full attention. "What are you talking about?" she asked.

"Pockets to let. That's what I'm saying. Your husband won't have a feather to fly with if he stays in Mr. Roker's company for long. I tell you, that Jack Sharp's eyes fair popped straight out his head when he clapped 'em on all that blunt your man was carrying."

Alexandria was horrified. "Do you mean that Mr. Roker is a gambler?"

"That's exactly wot I means. Separating Johnny Raws from their cash is by way of bein' his only trade. Not that he needs another, he's that good at wot he does."

"Oh, dear." Even to Alexandria's ears the expression seemed inadequate. The boots agreed that it missed the mark.

" 'Oh, dear' don't begin to cover it. You should've seen Mr. Roker when he saw your husband's blunt. Fairly drooled, that's wot he done. I hopes you personally hung on to enough of the ready to pay your shot, ma'am, because there's little likelihood your bridegroom can. That is, not unless," he added craftily, "you was to put a sudden stop to the fleecin' of the lamb yourself."

"How could I?" Alexandria tried to stop the question, but her panic would not allow it.

"I wouldn't like to say." Underneath the freckles and the blacking and the coal dust the young boots's face turned red. "But I don't expect the gentleman ever planned to be playing cards all night, seein' as how he was so recent wed. And it's not as if you was a lady a man would go out of his way to avoid." He stopped, turning redder still. "Wot I means to say is, I'm sure your husband didn't have much say in the matter once Mr. Roker picked him. That villain is slicker than a patch of goose grease and has a rare talent for having his own way. So I expect if you knocked on the parlor door and told your husband that it was bedtime, he'd be grateful."

"Oh, no, he would not be!"

The boots's expression showed what he thought of the strange customs of the upper class. "Queer kind of start I calls it—cards on his wedding night."

"But you could do it, though!" Alexandria suddenly brightened up. "You could interrupt the game and tell Mr. Romney that he's playing with a card sharp."

"Not bleedin' likely!" The boots was definitely alarmed. He was of diminutive proportions and looked as though he might only recently have been promoted from chimney sweep. "I could do that— warn your man, I mean—but you haven't seen the size of Mr. Roker, and that's a fact. And his friends is worse. They'd sooner break me arm as have their tea if they found out I'd tipped him. No, ma'am. I have to earn me livin' in these parts, while you're just passing through, like. *You* do it."

They stared at one another for a few moments,

obviously at an impasse. Then it was Alexandria's turn for inspiration. "I know," she said. "*You* go knock on Mr. Roker's door"— she held up a hand to stop the rush of protest—"and tell Mr. Romney that I rang the bell and you were the only one awake to answer."

"That's true enough," the bootblack said.

"And, say that I've been taken deathly ill. That way Mr. Roker can't possibly blame you for breaking up the game. And when I tell Harry that he was lured into the game by a professional card sharp, I don't think he'll be too angry." She said that last a little doubtfully. "You're quite sure Mr. Roker is a cheat?"

"His coat sleeves is too full o' cards to allow for shirt room," the boots answered solemnly.

"In that case, Harry should be grateful, even if he isn't."

"He'll be a lot richer, anyways. I just hope it ain't too late. Though I doubt he's skinned yet. That Mr. Roker's a crafty villain. Takes his own time about stealin' a man's eyeteeth. Don't want the victim to get suspicious, like."

"Well, then." Alexandria grasped the volume of sermons more as righteous armament than as reading matter. "Give me a few minutes to get back to my room. Then go fetch Mr. Romney."

"Wot shall I say is wrong?" The boots suddenly seemed to doubt his histrionic powers.

"The grippe!" Alexandria improvised. "I'm having chills and fever something awful. Mr. Romney will believe that, I'm sure."

"I certainly hope so." The young man seemed more and more doubtful about this route to a good night's sleep. "I certainly hope your husband believes me, for come to think on it, he looks as dangerous as Mr. Roker. I'd hate to get him into a taking, and that's the God's truth of it."

"If he does get into a taking, it won't be at you. And, anyhow, we've got to save him from getting—"

"Plucked?"

"Exactly. So let's get on with it."

In spite of all his qualms, the boots evidently played his part effectively. Alexandria had scarcely crawled into bed and pulled the curtains prudently around it before she heard hurried footsteps up the hall.

The Honorable Henry's door key grated in the lock.

Chapter
Seven

A LEXANDRIA TURNED HER FACE TOWARD THE WALL
and breathed as slowly and as deeply as she
could. As Harry jerked the bed curtains open, she
toyed with the idea of adding a snore for an artistic
touch, then rejected the notion as beyond her at the
moment.

"Alex?" Harry's voice was hoarse with anxiety.
"Alex, are you all right?"

Alexandria gave a low and, she thought, authentic moan. But it must have failed to carry conviction with it, for a calloused hand was laid none too gently on her head. "Fever be damned! You're cool as a cucumber."

A shiver seemed in order now, so she tried it. "Ow!" she protested and sat bolt upright as Harry's candle dripped tallow on her. "You did that on purpose!"

"I did not. But at least you now have your first true ailment. What the devil is this all about?" Mr. Romney was plainly miffed. "I told you I had no wish to sleep, and I can't believe that you're inviting me to your bed. Are you?"

"No, of course not," Alexandria said, a bit too hastily perhaps, judging from the speed with which her bridegroom's irritation turned to anger.

"Then why the devil did you see fit to interfere with the only diversion to be found in this godforsaken place? You did send the boots to fetch me, did you not? Or was that, too, merely a Banbury Tale on his part, along with your fatal illness?"

"That much was true," she admitted reluctantly. "I did send him."

"Why? Not that I really need to ask," he added in disgust.

"Because that diversion you referred to was a scheme to take your money."

"Playing piquet is always a scheme to take somebody's money. That's the whole purpose."

"But you don't understand. Mr. Roker is a card sharp."

"So?"

"I mean he's a professional. That's what the boots said. He makes his living by playing cards with Johnny Raws." Mr. Romney's black eyes sparked in the candlelight at her term. She went on hastily, "I thought you'd be grateful to me for finding this out and rescuing you from his clutches."

"You thought that, did you?" Harry's tone was not encouraging. "Just what in the name of God made you think I didn't know it? I'm hardly the flat you seem to think me. I knew the fellow was a sharp from the way he lured me in."

"And you still allowed yourself to be—"

"I told you, I was grateful for the diversion. This place is a dead bore, to put it mildly."

"And you were willing to play cards with a cheat and lose our means of getting back to London rather than—"

Harry was truly angry now. "Suppose you let me worry about our getting back to London? And as for my losing my blunt—I had no intention of it."

"If he cheats, how could you prevent it?"

"By pointing the fact out to him and persuading him to give up the practice."

"But the boots said—"

"I don't give a damn what the boots said. And furthermore, Alex, I don't mind saying that you're getting to be a cursed bore on the subject of card playing. Let me remind you once again, I cut my eye teeth some time ago. And I am not your father."

"Just the same, I could not conceive that you'd not appreciate a well-intended warning."

"Well, I don't," he interrupted brutally. "And let me advise you either to get back down underneath those covers or put on your pelisse. Even Harriette Wilson," he added, referring to England's best known Cyprian, whose patrons included some of the country's greatest names, "would feel immodest in the squire's daughter's gown."

Alexandria, who had forgotten all about the gown, suddenly clutched the sheet up to her chin while her bridegroom turned on his heel and slammed the dressing-room door with a total disregard for the other guests who might be trying to sleep.

The unnecessary clatter he made preparing himself for bed undoubtedly caused him not to hear the soft tapping on their chamber door. After a slight pause to give Harry the opportunity to answer it, Alexandria sighed and climbed out of bed and into her pelisse. It was just as well Harry did not hear, she thought, concluding that it must be the boots come back to have his palm greased. And it was for certain that Harry was in no mood to reward the lad for his part in the upset of the game. Pausing only to pick up the candle and her reticule, Alexandria opened the door a crack.

"Lord bless my soul, can this be Mrs. Romney? Why, it's a miracle!"

The huge gentleman who stood beaming on the threshold seemed at first glance to be all that was amiable. His enormous face was split by a smile that stretched from ear to ear. But the narrowed eyes were so lacking in any warmth as to make Alexandria barely able to control a shiver when she looked at him. For there was something menacing about the man, a force of personality more frightening than his size. Alexandria required no introduction but he made one nonetheless.

"Allow me to present myself. I'm Mr. Stanley Roker. I was having a friendly game of cards with your husband when the boots came in to say you'd been taken ill. Gave the impression that you were hovering at death's door, in fact. Quite alarmed, your bridegroom. He fairly bolted. Wouldn't even finish out the hand, so concerned he was." Mr. Roker looked pointedly about the room. "Where is the dear lad, by the by?"

"He went to fetch the doctor," Alexandria improvised, without stopping to consider why she lied. She was only thankful that the hall door opened away from the dressing room and prayed that

Harry would not reappear before she got rid of Mr. Roker.

"Did he now? It looks to me like he'll be getting the poor man out of his bed for nothing."

"I do hope so," Alexandria said. "But it's hard to tell. These spells come and go. My London doctor is at a loss to account for them. Quite befuddled, in fact. I hope the local physician can help me."

"Your condition comes and goes, does it?" Mr. Roker had lost his smile. And suddenly his voice increased substantially in volume while he practically pushed his way into the room. His eyes traveled swiftly around, then fastened upon the door of the dressing room. "It appears to me that yours is a most timely ailment. Coming and going so conveniently as it does. You can give your husband my compliments when he returns." His voice dripped with sarcasm. "And tell him Stanley Roker is really touched at his tender concern over his little bride." So saying, he gave Alexandria a bow that seemed more threatening than courteous and turned abruptly on his heel and left. Alexandria all but slammed the door behind him and turned the key thankfully in the lock.

"Of all the bird-witted, mutton-headed—" Words seemed to fail the Honorable Henry Romney as he emerged from the dressing room.

"Mr. Roker?"

"You, of course. How could you have been so stupid as to open the door? My God, I can't turn my back for a minute without having you landing us both in some kind of coil! Just for the record, do you always fling your door wide open in the middle of the night for any villain who might be standing there?"

"I thought it was the boots," she said defensively. "Besides, what harm did I do? So now he knows I wasn't ill. It serves him right. He's fleeced enough people in his time."

"That's just the point, my caper-witted lovely. After seeing you in such blooming health, Mr. Roker is convinced that I set him up with your connivance. He'd been playing me like a salmon. First wheedling me into the game, reluctant though I was, of course. Then allowing me to win the bigger part of the bank to keep me there. And just as he was about to reel me in and get his own back—plus everything I won right down to my borrowed shirt—I left. For your information, Alexandria, you don't walk out of a game of hazard when it's barely started and you've almost cleaned the pot, even if it's a friendly game. And I assure you, this was not."

"I'm certainly sorry that you were guilty of a breach of manners. But I still don't see why you're in such a taking. The man's a thief. It serves him right."

"The man is a thief. And he has a certain reputation to maintain." Harry's voice was grim. "Well, what's done's done. We might as well go to bed and save our candles, which obviously aren't of the all-night variety."

"Would you like to sleep in the bed?" Alexandria meekly tried to make amends.

"With you?" The bridegroom looked startled.

"No-no. I just meant I'd take the couch. It looks rather short for you."

"It does, for a fact."

Harry stared without enthusiasm at the window sofa. It was obviously a brand-new acquisition,

82

bought to add a touch of elegance to the inn's best bedchamber. It was not even five feet long, Alexandria estimated, and instead of having been constructed in the Grecian manner with one head rest, this was all symmetry, rising steeply at both ends like two headboards on a bed. It was a thing of beauty, upholstered in deep rose satin, framed in carved rosewood, decorated with panels of brass marquetry. But as a place for sleeping, especially for a man who measured well over six feet in height, Alexandria suspected it would have fit right into a medieval torture scheme.

"Do let me sleep there," she felt compelled to say again.

"No. For comfort it may leave a bit to be desired, but the location is excellent."

Upon Mr. Roker's exit Harry had emerged bootless from the dressing room with his huge shirt flapping around his biscuit pantaloons. He now proceeded to remove the shirt, and his bride found herself admiring the ripple of the muscles in his broad shoulders as he walked over to throw a few more coals upon the waning fire. His face was not nearly so handsome as Oliver's—she made the inevitable comparison—but she had to admit he had the better figure. It was all that boxing, she supposed.

At just that moment he walked over and jerked the counterpane ungallantly from over her. "I will take this," he said. "All those quilts will surely do you. If your bosom gets too chilled, just put on your pelisse." He gave the bed hangings a forceful tug and rang the curtain down, so to speak, on her view of the bedchamber. Then he blew out the candle. There was enough light, however, between the fireplace and the moon, to allow her to peep between the curtains and observe him trying to fold his lanky frame to fit the sofa. He swore once, savagely, as his head came into sudden contact with carved rosewood. Alexandria did not clap her hand over her mouth quite in time to muffle a giggle.

"Damn you, Mrs. Romney," the Honorable Henry said.

"Good night yourself," his bride answered him.

This time, exhaustion overtook Alexandria quickly and smothered any pangs of conscience she might have felt over the uncomfortable night Harry was doomed to spend. She was deep into a confused dream that had to do with Lady Augusta playing whist with Mr. Roker and rapping his knuckles with her fan for cheating, when the card game changed suddenly into a clash of armies with Harry leading a cavalry charge in the midst of muffled shouts and grunts and swearing and overturned furniture.

Furniture! Alexandria sat suddenly upright, wide awake. She opened the bed curtains a tiny crack and risked a peep, then nearly closed them once again. So unlikely was the sight she saw outlined in the dying firelight that she almost persuaded herself it was the continuation of the dream. Harry was thrashing on the floor, locked in mortal combat with a large assailant whose face she could not see but whose bulk identified him as Mr. Roker. The window was wide open, showing the method of his entry. The rosewood sofa was overturned and both combatants were entwined in the counterpane.

Alexandria knelt on the bed, her head protruding between the curtains, frozen in horror, and watched the two men struggle. Though no authority on the art of mayhem, Alexandria judged Harry the more fit and skillful of the two. But Mr. Roker outweighed him by several stone, a tremendous advantage, Alexandria noted with dismay as he gave Harry a heave that reversed their position and landed him on top. He was doing his utmost to go for Harry's throat, but was being temporarily prevented from it by Harry's two hands clamped upon his wrists, a state of affairs which could not last for long, considering that the bulk of Mr. Roker's enormous body must be pressing the breath right out of her husband. It was obvious that Harry needed help. Alexandria's first instinct was to leap for the bell pull. But her benumbed brain came alive enough to recall their distance from its source and the size of the little boots who would be the likely one to hear it. No—if Harry was to be saved from momentary annihilation, she, Alexandria, would have to do it. She was, after all, a Linnell. Her ancestors had fought the Crusades. With that ennobling thought, she snatched up the heavy candlestick from the nightstand and came leaping off the bed.

"Hold him still, Harry!" she screeched, swinging the japanned candlestick just as Harry had finally found the leverage to heave his hefty opponent off him. As the two combatants rotated, the candlestick, instead of finding its true target, the back of Mr. Roker's head, cracked sickeningly over Mr. Romney's eye.

"Ow!" he yelled and momentarily lost his hold, whereupon Mr. Roker flipped him like a coin and was on top again. "For God's sake, Alex, don't help me anymore."

Harry's bitter plea was muffled by the mass of Mr. Roker. But Alexandria heard and chose to ignore what could have been his last request. She swung the candlestick again, this time adding voice. "Help! Murder! Thief! Help! Somebody help us, please!" she screamed as the japanned candlestick beat a veritable tattoo upon the gambler's head and shoulders.

"Thief?" Mr. Roker managed to take exception to her scream while simultaneously holding Harry by the throat, partially ducking Alexandria's blows, and reaching into his waistcoat. "You've bloody little business calling an honest gambling man a thief after the little game you pulled!" At last he succeeded in withdrawing a wicked-looking pistol from the recesses of his coat and pointing it at Harry. "Now stiffle that caterwauling or I'll blow off your bridegroom's head. Not that he'd be much loss to you at that," he sneered. "Spending his honeymoon at cards and sleeping on a settee, so as a man can't even get through the bloody window to get his own back again. I've known a few queer, overbred coves in my time, but damme if you looked the type."

"Let's not be insulting," Harry managed to wheeze with the bit of air left in his lungs under the pressure of Mr. Roker.

"All right now," the gambler growled, starting to stand up. "I'll just take what I came for, thank you, and what's rightly mine, and be on my way before the inn comes down around my ears."

But he spoke too late, for suddenly they heard doors slamming and feet running down the hall. Mr. Roker swore violently and began backing toward the window, his pistol still leveled at Harry's head. "I ain't likely to forget this, Romney," he snarled just before he plunged down the ladder he'd placed there. The very last thing to disappear was Roker's pistol.

"Are you all right in there?" Alexandria recognized the shrill voice of the boots.

"Open up!" the landlord shouted. "For lord's sake, what's happening?"

Harry groaned and rose to a sitting position while Alexandria started for the door. "No!" he croaked.

"What?"

"I'll do it, for God's sake!" With great difficulty he staggered toward the door and opened it a crack.

"What's going on in there?" the frightened landlord asked.

"Nothing. Nothing at all to be alarmed about." Harry's voice was soothing. "It's our honeymoon, you know." He grinned sheepishly. "The bride got a bit carried away, that's all. Sorry we disturbed you."

"My God!" the bootblack breathed.

"What on earth possessed you to say an odious thing like that?" Alexandria exploded after Harry had tipped the landlord and the bootblack generously with Roker's money and had closed the door.

"Just trying to restore my self-esteem after Roker's insinuations, that's all."

"I don't even know what you're talking about." Alexandria feared that the beating he'd just taken had unhinged his reason.

"I know you don't. But let's not talk about it right now. Instead, would you do me one small favor?" He rubbed his head gingerly where the candlestick had hit it.

She felt her face flame with remorse and guilt. "Of course, Harry. Anything you say."

"Put on that damn pelisse."

At first Alexandria considered the request one more sign of possible dilerium. But then she glanced down to discover that the squire's daughter's gown had, indeed, lost its moorings during the struggle with Roker, exposing her bosom shamelessly. With a gasp she leaped for the pelisse and put it on.

"That's better," Harry said. "After the drubbing my manhood's just taken, there's no use flaunting that temptation at me. This is no time to try and redeem myself."

Chapter
Eight

*T*HE NEXT MORNING ALEXANDRIA WAS INCLINED TO think that she had dreamed it all. The sofa sat sedately where it belonged, and there was no sign of Harry.

Harry! She sat up in some alarm and listened for sounds of stirring in the dressing room. Silence. The clock on the mantel broke it by striking seven. She jumped out of bed, shrugged into her pelisse, and prepared to go for help. At that moment the lock turned and Harry entered from the hall.

"Oh, thank goodness!"

His eyebrows shot up from the effusiveness of her greeting, a gesture that he obviously regretted from the way he winced. His face was not prepossessing. The blow from the japanned candlestick had done more than raise a goose egg; it had discolored his flesh and almost closed one eye.

"I take it you're glad to see me," he said, closing the door behind him. "Why?"

"I was afraid something terrible had happened to you."

"It has." His voice was bitter as he touched his forehead gingerly.

"Not that—though I am terribly sorry, I truly am. I had meant to help. And you must admit that I did help in the end."

"I suppose so," he admitted grudgingly.

"Suppose? There is no doubt. But that was not what I meant about something terrible happening. I meant that when I woke up and saw that you were gone, I was afraid Mr. Roker had murdered you."

"No. I think he prefers to leave that sort of thing to you." Evidently, Harry had no intention of letting her forget her misplaced blow. "At least, he's left the inn," Harry went on. "One step ahead of the law, I understand. They want to settle some old scores with him. But never mind Roker now. Hurry up and get ready to leave, Alexandria."

She looked at him uneasily. The proper use of her first name seemed to indicate displeasure with her and disenchantment with their arrangement. "I've bespoken breakfast," he continued. "We'll make an early start."

He left her then, and she did, indeed, hurry through her toilet. Alexandria felt it would be prudent not to keep her husband waiting.

The remainder of their wedding journey was uneventful. Harry kept to the routine that he'd begun, sleeping throughout the day during the coach ride and finding whatever amusement might be available when they stopped. Alexandria took care not to inquire as to the nature of his diversions. Once she suspected that he'd gone to view a local boxing match that she'd overheard discussed. But even though she ranked that so-called sport almost as low as gambling, she kept her lips sealed tight upon the subject. She hoped that she was learning tact where her new husband was concerned. For there was no doubt in her mind that he already regretted his impetuosity in wedding her.

She had known, of course, that this state of affairs was inevitable, but she had not expected it to overtake Harry quite so soon. And she deeply regretted it.

For, in contrast, Alexandria was experiencing an almost euphoric sense of freedom. And her gratitude to Harry increased with every mile that separated her from Lady Augusta and her former life. Travelling with Harry had restored her self-respect. It was marvelous to be catered to once more, to be taken for a person of consequence instead of a nobody, neither quality nor servant, barely tolerated on the fringes of an employer's social world.

Indeed, she thought, as they finally drove into London, the past three days had been the best she had known since her father's death. Even the ache in her throat that arose unbidden when she thought of Oliver, now lost to her forever, could not mar her pleasure in her new position. What did threaten to spoil it was Harry's obvious discontent. Well, she'd make that up to him, Alexandria vowed as the coach turned into Edgeware Road. Here in London she would be all that was amiable. And never, never would she meddle in Harry's life again.

The carriage came to a stop in Grosvenor Square. Harry, roused from his slumbers, yawned inelegantly while Alexandria pressed her nose against the window glass and gawked. "Do you live here?" she asked, trying but failing to keep her voice casual.

"This is my house," he replied. "Actually, I'm here very little, but you'll be staying here."

"It's a terribly fashionable address, is it not?" she blurted out, feeling quite countrified.

"Yes, I suppose it is," he answered carelessly, handing her out of the carriage and escorting her up the marble steps. "It was part of my inheritance from my Uncle Adolphus. He was a stickler for such things."

The door was opened by a short, elderly butler, equipped with the imperturbability of his trade. If he saw anything at all odd in his master's unkempt appearance or in his battered face or in the young lady with him wearing the dowdy, travel-tired pelisse, he did not show it. "Welcome home, sir," was his only comment.

"Alexandria, this is Padgett. He's been here for donkeys' years. First with my uncle, now with me. Padgett, this is my bride, Mrs. Romney, the former Miss Linnell of Rose Hall, Westmorland." The introduction was quite offhand, as if Harry brought brides into his household every day. And, indeed, from the butler's demeanor, it might well have been his custom. The servant bowed his welcome to Alexandria and gave his congratulations to Harry without the slightest alteration in his expression. He then ushered the bride to a bedchamber as though she had been in residence for years.

Alexandria, however, wished there had been time

for Padgett to give her lessons in impassivity. She felt her chin drop. It was all she could do to cut off her gasp. She had been raised in an atomophere of genteel shabbiness. And, while Lady Augusta had not lacked for money, she was naturally bent toward parsimony. By contrast, the furnishings of the room which they were entering seemed lavish enough to suit a prince's taste. The enormous four-poster bed was made of carved gilt wood, surmounted by a golden dome, and hung with curtains and valances of painted silk.

Harry saw her eyes grow wide as she looked at it. "Uncle Adolphus was misplaced in life. He would have liked to have been an eastern potentate." He smiled as though in fond memory.

Alexandria's awestruck gaze went travelling from the bed to the rosewood banded dressing table to the towering wardrobe in the Egyptian style. There was a cheval glass with carved Egyptian figures on the standards, and a Grecian-style couch inlaid with ornamental brass that made the one that Harry had slept on on their wedding night seem shabby by comparison. She hoped that her mouth was not still ajar.

"Is it to your satisfaction?" The amusement in Harry's voice destroyed that hope.

"Oh, yes, quite satisfactory," she managed at last to say.

"Very well, then," he said. "That should be that." And he moved toward the door.

Alexandria looked at his retreating back with a sense of panic. What should be what? she wanted to call after him, but remembered the butler's presence just in time.

At the doorway, Harry paused and turned around.

"Oh, damn," he said. "I suppose we should go to see my father as soon as possible. I'll just pop over to Marylebone New Road and make myself presentable. I'll call back for you in about an hour."

"And just how, in the meantime, do I make myself presentable?" Alexandria replied quietly.

"Damn," he said again. His vocabulary seemed to be temporarily stuck. "I'll find someone to take you round the shops tomorrow. But I don't think we can put off calling on my father till your wardrobe's ready. Word of our marriage is bound to spread like wildfire, and he'd best hear it from me first.

"You couldn't just wear what you have on, I suppose? No, I guess you couldn't. Never mind. I'll fetch you something. Feed her, Padgett, and I'll be back by four. We should be able to catch my father at home."

Padgett hurried off to give orders for a nuncheon to be prepared and to send a goggle-eyed maid up to attend to the new mistress.

But after her hasty bath, Alexandria was unable to eat the food thoughtfully provided on a tray, "so as not to keep the master waiting." She was panicked at the notion of being presented to Lord Woolridge without warning as his son's new wife. She had met that gentleman during her childhood but recalled him only dimly. What she did remember was not encouraging. A tall man, aloof and very dignified. And there was nothing she had learned about him since to make her anticipate any but the coolest of receptions, if, indeed, he did not turn them away from the door.

True, her family was as good as his, Alexandria tried to reassure herself. But that could not erase the fact that she'd gone from governess to lady's companion and, worst of all, eloped in such a shocking manner to Gretna Green. Her cheeks flamed hot as she realized that Lord Woolridge's, and indeed all of society's, first conclusion would be that his son was forced by necessity to marry her. They'd soon find they were mistaken on that count. But in the meantime Lord Woolridge would think that his scapegrace son had married a female very wanting in conduct, indeed.

Coinciding with this lowering thought, Maggie, the fifteen-year-old maid assigned to her, came rushing into the room with a huge, untidy brown paper bundle and a hatbox in her hand. "Mr. Romney said to fetch this to you," she said breathlessly, "and for you to hurry up and dress." She colored as she realized it would have been more tactful not to quote her master quite so literally. "He's waiting in the library, if you please, Madam."

Alexandria quickly took the bundle, trying not to wonder who had wrapped it so messily. While Maggie gave an "Oh!" of appreciation, she pulled out a pale green walking dress, obviously quite expensive and obviously of the very latest style. A bonnet of a slightly darker green trimmed with a lighter plume of ostrich feathers was in the box, along with some matching green kid gloves.

With Maggie's help Alexandria quickly put on the dress. Then she surveyed herself in the cheval glass and groaned.

"It is a bit largish, Madam," Maggie remarked sympathetically.

"Yes. And from the look of it it might have been made for the squire's daughter. Only I'll bet a monkey this squire's daughter has red hair."

"Beg pardon, Madam?"

"Never mind. But I certainly can't go out like this. We'll just have to alter it."

"But the master's in a terrible rush, Mrs. Romney."

"I'm sorry about that, but I'm not going into Lord Woolridge's presence tripping on my skirt if I can help it. Fetch me a needle and thread, please, Maggie."

Thirty minutes later, after some rapid stitching on her part and a hasty application of the smoothing iron on Maggie's, she joined her husband in the library looking as though the dress might possibly have been made for her, although with little regard for her coloring.

Harry rose from his seat behind the desk and looked her critically up and down. "That did very well," he congratulated himself. "I was afraid it might be a little large—er, here and there."

"It was," she answered briefly. "I can see you've been reunited with your valet."

He was wearing snowy linen, a dark blue coat, buff pantaloons, and Hessian boots with a mirror-finish shine. "Yes," he agreed, grinning. "After I revived him from his faint, he brought me right back up to snuff, wouldn't you say?"

"Oh, yes. You are a tulip of fashion at the very least."

"That just goes to show you've never seen one. Shall we go? I thought we'd walk. It's only a short distance to my father's place."

They trudged in silence for a bit, with Alexandria completely occupied at first with gawking at the grand houses and the other strollers and the carriages and the chairs in this, her first taste of London. Suddenly she chuckled.

Harry looked quizzically down his crooked nose. "What do you find amusing?"

"I'd rather not say, if you don't mind."

"Indeed? Why not?"

"I don't think you'd find it funny."

"Try me."

"Well, then, I was just wondering what possible explanation you could have given when you borrowed these clothes I'm wearing from your—uh—friend."

"Oh, that. Why, that was no problem," Harry assured her, solemn-faced. "I simply told my mistress I needed an outfit for my wife."

As Alexandria went off into a bout of uncontrollable laughter, the Honorable Henry frowned his disapproval. "You're quite right," he said. "I fail to see the humor."

Chapter Nine

HARRY HAD TIMED THEIR ARRIVAL IN BROOK STREET to be after the proper hours for social calls and before Lord Woolridge sat down to his dinner. But as they were being ushered upstairs, they heard the murmur of conversation. "Is my mother-in-law at home?" Harry asked the butler in some surprise.

"No, sir. Lady Woolridge and her children are still in the country. Sir Oliver and Lady Linnell are with his lordship."

"Oh, my God," Harry groaned underneath his breath. "Don't bother to announce us, Albert." And, grabbing Alexandria by the arm, he strode purposefully toward the door.

For a moment Alexandria lost touch with reality as their sudden appearance upon the threshold seemed to turn the occupants of the parlor to stone. Lady Amelia Fielding—no, Linnell, Alexandria had to remind herself—faced their way, and she was the one who saw them first. She halted her tea cup halfway to her mouth with a look of astonishment upon her face.

Lord Woolridge, seated on the opposite side of the fireplace from Amelia, turned their way also, and gave them a scarcely welcoming appraisal through his quizzing glass.

Alexandria's eyes finally sought Oliver. He'd been lounging against the mantelpiece but now he stood upright and the hand that held his tea cup shook enough for it to rattle. His eyes were riveted upon Alexandria's face and his expression could best be described as stricken.

Lord Woolridge, characteristically, recovered first. He rose slowly to his feet and turned toward his son. Alexandria dragged her gaze from Oliver to look closely at Harry's father.

The first impression was startling, as though Oliver had suddenly aged right before her eyes. No wonder Lord Woolridge preferred his nephew to his son, she thought. Oliver, in looks at least, was he himself made over.

"And to what do we owe this unexpected pleasure, Henry?" Lord Woolridge did not look particularly overjoyed. After the initial glance her way, he seemed determined to ignore Alexandria's presence.

"I had thought to find you alone, sir," Harry answered, with more truth than tact. "I have come to make my bride known to you."

Their entrance had been a shock; this announcement was cataclysmic. Lady Amelia gasped, Oliver's tea cup danced a jig, and Lord Woolridge dropped his quizzing glass. "Is this one of your tasteless jokes?" he inquired icily.

"Indeed no, sir," Harry answered. "May I present my wife, the former Alexandria Linnell? She is, of course, a cousin to Oliver and acquainted with the new Lady Linnell." He bowed slightly in their direction.

"Alexandria, how could you—" Oliver began in a choked voice before recollecting himself and stopping short. But he hadn't the strength to conceal the misery on his face. Alexandria was dimly aware of Amelia's shocked expression and Harry's mocking amusement as they both stared at him. Alexandria, who had tried hard to forget her loss, now felt her own heart near to breaking. He should not have had to learn of her marriage this way. It was too cruel.

Lord Woolridge, the politician, quickly regained his poise. "Come and sit down." He ushered them into the room, indicating a sofa near the fire where they sat together, for all the world like prisoners in the dock. "You are Jarrell Linnell's daughter?" The question was asked politely. Perhaps Alexandria only imagined that he was mentally reviewing her father's sad and disgraceful history.

"Yes, I am," she answered.

"Alex was serving as companion to Lady Augusta," Harry volunteered. He stretched his long legs out in front of him, crossing his gleaming Hessians at the ankles. Though his face was expressionless, Alexandria had the impression he was suddenly enjoying the situation. "We'd known each other as infants, of course," he continued, while his father's stony stare never left his face. "But, as I re-

100

marked to Oliver, I was quite unprepared for the change in her."

"It was love at first sight then, I take it?" his father remarked dryly.

"Yes, and coming on the heels of your many hints that it was time I wed, it did seem fortuitous. Lucky thing for me, sir, your suggesting I go visit the great-aunt. Would never have met Alex otherwise."

Amelia Linnell shot Harry a look laced with venom and Oliver gave him a quelling glare. But Lord Woolridge, perhaps more accustomed to sparring with his son, refused to acknowledge any hit.

"That's all very well, I'm sure," he said. "But it still fails to explain why you had to marry in this furtive manner. Gretna Green, I take it?"

"Nor does it explain who hit you," Oliver interrupted. Up to that point everyone had tactfully avoided staring at, let alone mentioning, Harry's discolored eye. But Oliver was far too agitated to stand on ceremony. It was obvious that he considered Harry's battered appearance the only bright spot of the day.

"Well," Harry drawled, taking a slow measure of his cousin, "the fact is that somehow or other our aged relative got wind of the fact that I intended to abduct her pet slave and landed me a facer in order to stop it. Oh, you find that hard to believe, do you, cousin?" he inquired as Oliver's face became even more suffused with anger. "Well, then, how about this version—Alexandria hit me."

"You—you—despicable—"

But instead of allowing Oliver to produce the exact descriptive word to fit his character, Harry turned once more to face his father. "To answer your question, sir, we did go to Gretna Green." He showed neither contrition nor embarrassment. "The knot is as well and truly tied as would have been done at St. Paul's Cathedral. And I do dislike a fuss."

"I'm well aware of that. However, it would have been considerate to think of the possible effect upon your family. But no more of that." He smiled his chilly smile once more. "We will change the subject from your nuptials to your future. What are your plans?"

"Plans?" Harry looked at his father blankly, as if the word were totally new to him.

"Forgive me." Lord Woolridge's sarcasm was of the light variety. "I can see I've caught you quite unprepared. Tactless of me, I'm sure. But, since I was just discussing Oliver's future with him, I fear my mind involuntarily kept to the same course."

"Oliver has just accepted a post as Lord Woolridge's secretary," Lady Linnell smugly interposed.

"Secretary is simply a title of convenience," his lordship went on to say. "The fact is, Oliver is desirous of a political career and we felt that assisting me would be a good way to begin. We should both profit from the association. I think Oliver shows a tremendous aptitude for the world of politics."

"Does he, by Jove?" Harry drawled. "I can't say, though, that I'm surprised. Look at his choice of father-in-law."

Lady Linnell seemed not to know whether to be pleased or insulted. Oliver had no doubt. But Lord Woolridge chose to ignore his son's aside altogether.

"I don't mind admitting that I had hoped that you . . ." he began, then his voice trailed off with the merest of sighs. "But then we can't all be fascinated by government, can we, Mrs. Romney?" He gave Alexandria a frigid smile.

"We can be involved as mere citizens without having a desire for office," Alexandria said stoutly. "Harry, for instance, seems more fascinated"— she gave the same stress to the word that Lord Woolridge had—"by farming. I find his views on the new agriculture quite interesting. And, considering the impact the corn laws are having, as a landowner he may have as much influence in the long run as you and Oliver." She felt her face turn red as everyone stared at her in astonishment, Harry most of all. Even Lord Woolridge lost a bit of his aplomb.

"I should, indeed, be fascinated to hear your views," he said to his son with lightly veiled sarcasm.

Harry merely shrugged. "Would you, sir? Would you really be tempted to discontinue your support of the corn laws if I demonstrated how improvement in farm methods would make your restrictions unnecessary, not to say immoral?"

There was an awkward silence. Then Amelia's superior breeding prompted her to ask, "Where will you be living?" She directed the question toward Alexandria, but Harry answered.

"Grosvenor Square. And you?"

Even before Amelia answered, Alexandria surmised that theirs was a more fashionable location than the newlywed Linnells'.

"On Wimpole Street. Temporarily, at least. Good property is so difficult to find just now, you know."

"Indeed. I am fortunate that mine has been in the family," Harry murmured.

Alexandria felt another urge to giggle. This

abominable habit seemed to be growing on her, the result, no doubt, of nervous stress.

There was another silence, and this time Alexandria sought to bridge it. "Have you completed the scene you were embroidering?" she inquired politely of Amelia.

She had merely meant to make conversation, she told herself, not to give Amelia a set-down for her former rudeness. Indeed, she told herself, she had quite forgotten that incident until Amelia's face flamed red and Oliver gave her a reproachful look.

"How long have you been in town?" Lord Woolridge said, to the next pause.

"We've only just arrived," Harry answered him.

"And is this your first visit to the metropolis?" He turned his polite and distant gaze upon Alexandria.

"Yes, it is, sir."

"Then you shall enjoy seeing the sights. My son should excel in introducing you to society. No one knows the frivolous life as well as he."

If he expected a reply from Alexandria, he was disappointed. She pressed her lips tightly together and said nothing, though she was surprisingly annoyed at the way Lord Woolridge had slurred his son.

"Oliver was so fortunate as to obtain vouchers to Almack's for us," Amelia said, giving her husband a smug smile. "They are quite difficult to come by, you know."

Indeed, Alexandria did know. The fame of that social club had spread even to the provinces. Almack's was known to be severely restrictive as to those it admitted to its balls. Persons in trade need not apply, no matter how much wealth they had accumulated. Girls new to the fashionable world suffered the agonies of the damned when unable to make the exclusive list.

Male guests not only had to be impeccable as to background, they must also be accomplished dancers and dress in the proper knee britches and white cravats. Even the great Wellington had been turned away from the door at Almack's when he sought admittance clad in trousers.

"Would you care to go? To Almack's, I mean?" Harry asked his bride. Obviously the idea had not previously occurred to him.

"Of course she would like to go," his father said impatiently. "Who would not wish it?"

"Any number of people, I should think. I always found the place a dead bore myself. Lemonade and tea, stale cake, bread and butter. But if you think you'd like it, Alex . . ."

"Yes, I think I should," his bride answered diffidently, hoping that this stated preference for high society did not run counter to her resolution not to cause her bridegroom any further inconvenience.

"Perhaps Oliver could—"

Harry interrupted Amelia's condescension. "No need to trouble my cousin. I'll ask the princess."

"You are acquainted with Princess Esterhazy?" In spite of herself, Lady Linnell sounded impressed.

"My son is intimately acquainted with all the Almack patronesses. Indeed, he is quite at home in the world of the ton, I'm given to understand."

It occurred to Alexandria for the first time that perhaps there was some nuance of envy in Lord Woolridge's voice. And she wondered if the scapegrace son occupied a more secure social position than did the politician father.

"And speaking of that frivolous world," Harry

said, rising to his feet, "I am due shortly at Watier's. So I think we had best be going, Alex."

"Surely now that you are married you do not intend to fritter away your time in a club that is, by any other name, a gambling hell?" Lord Woolridge frowned, rising to his feet with Alexandria.

"White's and Watier's would both be forced to close their doors if all the married men stayed home," his son replied.

"Even so, it hardly seems proper to desert your bride on her first evening in town."

"It's no more than one might expect, however," Oliver said between clenched teeth.

"Oh, come now, Oliver," Harry replied pleasantly. "Don't try to pretend you really want me in Alex's pocket. I suggest you keep your disapproval for other areas of my life."

"Well, Alexandria," Lord Woolridge smoothly interposed. "I may call you that, may I not? I am counting on you to be a steadying influence upon Henry, a transformation, I realize, it would be unfair to expect you to accomplish overnight. I am grateful, however, to find that my son for once took my advice to heart and has found himself a bride." She did not miss the irony in his tone that made it evident he realized that Harry had gone to considerable pains to avoid the bride of his father's choosing. "This compliance on his part must be a first where our relationship is concerned. Who knows what may come of it. Why, any time now he may come seeking my advice in other areas of his life.

"Are you sure your business at Watier's cannot wait until after we dine together, Harry?" his father continued. "Amelia and Oliver are staying. I will tell Albert to lay extra covers."

106

Harry, however, declined the invitation, a circumstance that did not seem to distress his father overmuch. As Lord Woolridge took Alexandria's hand to kiss it, his son remembered to take his formal leave of his cousin's bride. Seeing Harry thus occupied, Oliver seized the chance to walk Alexandria to the parlor door.

"Oh, Alexandria, how could you? How could you possibly have married that—that—" he demanded.

"Don't!" She put a stop to any name-calling. "I'll not allow you to speak ill of Harry. I owe him far too much. And as for why I married him, you of all people should not have to ask."

Their whispered conversation was cut short by Harry's approach. Oliver seized Alexandria's hand and lingered over it a bit longer perhaps than decreed by etiquette or appreciated by his own bride. At last Harry felt constrained to clear his throat and take Alexandria by the elbow. The goodbyes then became more general and Mr. and Mrs. Romney soon found themselves on Brook Street.

Alexandria breathed a sigh of heartfelt relief. "Thank goodness that is over. But it was not half so bad as I had feared. Or did you not think so?"

"It had its ugly moments," Harry muttered.

"Why, whatever do you mean? I thought, all things considered, your father was quite civil. True, he does seem to feel compelled to give you a setdown upon the slightest provocation. Is that what you refer to?"

"No. I'm quite accustomed to his set-downs. They seldom bother me. What did disturb me was that you felt compelled to enter the lists in my defense. 'Harry's views on the new agricultural methods are quite fascinating,'" he mimicked. "Of all the fustian. If you wish to concoct Banbury Tales about your own experiences, pray do so. But leave me out of it."

"I only wished—"

"I know what you wished—to make me sound as worthy as dear Oliver," he said viciously. "But I'll tell you right now, Alexandria, I will not be measured against his standard."

"No, I can see that that would be most improper," she retorted frigidly.

"It would indeed."

They proceeded for a while in silence. Alexandria broke it. "This has turned out quite badly for you, has it not?" she said.

"What do you mean?"

"I mean our marriage. It did not upset your father, I fear, nearly so much as you had hoped."

He thought about it for a few moments as they turned into Grosvenor Square. "That's true," he finally replied. "But, on the other hand, it bothered Cousin Oliver far beyond my wildest dreams. So that, at least, is something on the credit side."

Chapter
Ten

THE HONORABLE HENRY ROMNEY HAD EVIDENTLY had his fill of the married state. After the duty call upon his father, he deposited Alexandria in Grosvenor Square, but did not take up residence there himself. As to his precise location, Alexandria prudently did not inquire.

Harry did, however, recall his marital obligation long enough to send his business manager around the next day to arrange an allowance for Alexandria that caused that lady to gasp in protest, "Why, it's far too much!"

The lawyer looked at her in some surprise. This was not the type of comment usually heard. "Mr. Romney can well afford it," he assured her, before going on to explain that her husband did not intend the allowance to cover her clothing and household expenses. All those bills should be sent to him.

No sooner had he left than Alexandria sallied forth dressed in the borrowed walking dress, with Harry's footman in her wake, intent upon visiting London's smartest shops. Guided from one to the other by the surprisingly knowledgeable servant, she revelled in a profusion of satins and brocades, Indian muslins, tippets of fur and feathers, plumes, ribbons, lace, and other fancy trimmings in the latest mode.

Then she sought out a French dressmaker on Bruton Street who, so the footman, now laden with her purchases, had assured her, catered to the very pink of the ton, though how the young man came to know a thing like that was more than she could guess. But once she saw the smartness of the establishment and the obvious modishness of its clients, she did not doubt that he was right.

Alexandria was slightly overwhelmed when the proprietress, upon learning her identity, fobbed off an officious-looking lady and came to wait on her. After an hour spent in happy consultation, concluded by arrangements being made for the fittings, Alexandria, with the exhausted footman still in tow, moved on to burden him even further with large boxes from the milliners and smaller parcels from an emporium which had provided excellent bargains in silk stockings and French gloves.

It was an almost perfect day for the young matron, who had known the pinch of poverty all her life. Only one thing marred it. Alexandria was busily engaged in Layton & Shear's trying to choose between striped poplin and sprigged muslin, while in the back of her mind retaining the delicious thought that she could actually afford to buy them both, when she became aware of being stared at by a young woman two aisles away.

Her first thought was of the woman's vibrant loveliness, her flaming tresses, milky complexion, and eyes of emerald green. Alexandria thought her, without a doubt, the most striking female she had ever seen.

But a second impression followed so quickly that it blotted out the first. For the young woman's perfect features were marred by hostility. Alexandria turned her head, vainly expecting to see someone standing behind her, the object of the beauty's hateful glare. Then, when she looked back once more, she saw to her relief that the angry young woman was striding from the shop. All at once she understood—and felt her cheeks grow hot. The beauty was Harry's mistress, and she had recognized her clothes.

It was very lowering, of course, to be picked out of a crowd by a fashionable impure because you happened to be wearing her walking dress. It was also very lowering to find that your husband was giving carte blanche to a female whose beauty made you look absolutely drab by comparison. But Alexandria resolutely pushed the incident from her mind. Harry had warned her that their matrimonial bargain would not always be to her liking. It was time, perhaps, that she entered something on her ledger's debit side. So far the inconveniences of their alliance had been entirely his.

The encounter had nothing to do, she told herself, with the fact that for the next few days she was decidedly blue-deviled. Rather, her downcast spirits were the result of the strain of her elopement followed by an unaccustomed isolation. She found herself almost, but not quite, missing those quarrelsome games of chess with Lady Augusta, when she had pointed out the old woman's sly shifting of the pieces.

No one had come to call. Although the notice of the marriage of Miss Linnell and Mr. Romney had been duly inserted in the *Gazette*—by Lord Woolridge, not Harry, she suspected—it had brought no visitors to her door. She could only conclude that Harry's London acquaintances were either aware of the true nature of their marriage or else felt it tactful not to intrude upon their early wedded bliss. She could not decide which state of affairs felt the more lowering.

It became more and more apparent that Harry had meant what he had said. He desired a wife in name only, one who would not affect his accustomed lifestyle. After providing for her needs, he had obviously dismissed her from his thoughts.

Not that she minded that, of course. In fact, she was most relieved by the circumstances, she told herself, except that it made her situation rather awkward. She especially disliked the pity she thought she could detect in the servants' eyes.

The main problem was, there was very little an unescorted lady could do in the metropolis. Alexandria had had her fill of shopping, and there were only so many trips one could make to the circulating library. She thought with longing of the country and the long tramps she might take there. Perhaps she should write a note to Harry. Would the red-haired beauty read it? Could she read? Literacy was hardly a requirement for that profession, she thought cattishly. She would find out what he might think of her removing to his Westmorland house. It might be easier to make a life for herself in the country. London was obviously impossible.

While she fully appreciated Harry's need for freedom, it would have been nice if he'd remembered the voucher he'd promised to obtain for Almack's. But then, perhaps he had remembered and been refused. The rackety circumstances of their marriage might well have placed her quite beyond the pale. Besides, even if she had a voucher, she had no escort. Depressed by these and other lowering thoughts, she was headed down to peruse once more the contents of Harry's Irish uncle's library when she practically collided with a young man who was racing up the stairs.

He checked his three-risers-at-once lope just in the nick of time. "I say, who are you?" he blurted, setting down the portmanteau he carried.

She took a moment before answering, rendered speechless both by his sudden appearance and by his exquisiteness. Harry had been right, she realized, when he'd said that labeling him a tulip of fashion merely proved she'd never seen one. It was obvious that here was the real article indeed.

The stripling staring at her with such curiosity— surely he could be no more than seventeen—was wearing pantaloons of a bright canary yellow, Hessians that gleamed brighter still, a sky-blue coat nipped tightly at the waist and generously padded at the shoulders to make the contrast between the two more striking than nature had provided for. His shirt points were so high and so stiffly starched as to impede the turning of his head. His neck cloth fell gracefully into an intricate waterfall. The attention momentarily attracted by an enormous buttonhole was quickly reclaimed by a profusion of rings and fobs and chains.

The young man was sizing Alexandria up with as much intensity as she accorded him. And he evidently approved of what he saw. His blue eyes sparkled and his amiable countenance, only slightly marred by an adolescent spot or two, broke into an impish grin. "Oh, I say, am I supposed to know you?"

" 'Nay answer me,' " Alexandria retorted automatically. " 'Stand and unfold thyself.' "

"Oh, I say, that's Hamlet, isn't it? Wouldn't Old Hobson turn up his toes if he knew I'd recognized it. But to answer you, I'm Evelyn." Since, judging from Alexandria's puzzled look, that hardly seemed sufficient explanation, he enlarged upon the theme. "Evelyn Combe. Harry's brother-in-law. My mother's by way of being married to his father, don't you know."

"Oh, yes, of course," she answered, the light beginning now to dawn as she realized she was face to face with the deceased Earl of Chatsworth's second son.

"But you haven't 'unfolded' yourself," he continued. "Are you Harry's mis—No, you can't be." He colored with embarrassment. If he had known how young it made him look after all his efforts toward sophistication, he would have been still more mortified. "Impossible, of course. Shakespeare and all."

"Well, as to that," Alexandria replied thoughtfully, "I don't know that there's any stipulation against a light-skirt knowing Shakespeare. But you're right, in any case—I can't be. I'm Harry's wife."

Mr. Combe's jaw dropped, to its peril, threatening to impale itself upon his shirt points. "You can't be!" he exclaimed.

"Oh, come now." Alexandria, though on the whole rather drawn toward the impetuous stripling, felt just a bit annoyed. "You simply cannot go on insisting that I can't be this or that. I have to be something, you know, and the choices are not endless."

"Oh, dear," Mr. Combe said in such a stricken voice that it immediately wiped out Alexandria's irritation. "I have put my foot in it, haven't I? It's just that it's such a shock—surprise, I mean. I just cannot imagine Harry being legshackled—married, I mean to say. Though if I did imagine it," he said, trying valiantly to mend his fences, "you would be the perfect choice, of course."

Alexandria smiled at his horrendous struggle for diplomacy, and the young man looked enormously relieved. He grinned his engaging grin once more. "I say, what are you called? Besides Mrs. Romney, I mean to say."

"Alexandria," she answered him. "I was, till recently, Alexandria Linnell."

"Oh, and are you related then to Oliver Linnell?" Was it imagination, or did she detect a slight drop in the young man's cordiality?

"A cousin," she replied, then changed the subject. "Perhaps we should remove ourselves from the staircase, and then you can tell me what brings you into town. I collect you have only just arrived." She gestured toward the portmanteau.

As though on cue, Padgett appeared to take the bag and greet the young man as effusively as his position would allow. "Shall I take this to Master Evelyn's usual room, ma'am?" he inquired.

"Certainly," she answered, with only the tiniest constraint creeping into her voice. But Evelyn did not fail to notice it.

"Oh, I say," he said when they had been settled in the morning room with tea, "I do hope I won't be in the way. I mean to say, it is awfully nervy of me," he blushed, "with you so newly wed and all. I can go straight to my stepfather. As a matter of fact, that's where my mother thinks I have gone." He gave a sheepish grin. "I got so fed up with the country I thought I'd go berserk if I had to spend another week there. So I cut a wheedle and talked her into letting me come up to London. She rather has the idea that I'm interested in visiting Parliament and sitting at stepfather's feet and all. But actually I always stay with Harry when I can. He doesn't seem to mind. And it's ever so much jollier. But of course I'll understand if you—"

"I would love to have you stay," she hastened to reassure him, for he looked like a puppy about to be cast out of doors for chewing on a chair leg. "But the thing is, you see, Harry's not at home."

"He isn't?" Evelyn seemed to find this rather odd.

"He's away on business," Alexandria improvised. No one could accuse her of a whisker there, she thought.

"Gone to see about his holdings, has he? I'm not surprised. Harry's a very conscientious landlord. Most people think he's a care-for-nothing, but that simply isn't so. Well, you'd know that better than I would, wouldn't you?" He stopped his encomium in embarrassment. "I'm sure he's talked to you about the new agricultural theories he's put into practice at Gadsden. I say, are you quite all right?" Mr. Combe seemed at a loss as to whether or not he should slap Alexandria on the back, as she suddenly succumbed to a choking fit.

There was one thing Alexandria was sure of as she gradually recovered with the aid of the tea held to her lips by Evelyn. Though Harry Romney had few admirers among his family, his stepmama's second son was an enthusiastic exception to this rule.

"Well, I'd best be going, I expect," Mr. Combe remarked, once he'd finished his last crumb of bread and butter and Alexandria's also. "Since Harry is not at home, you know."

"Oh, please stay." The words slipped out impulsively, but Alexandria could not regret them as she observed Mr. Combe's expressive face light up. "I know it will be dull for you with Harry not here, but you would be doing me a tremendous favor. You see, I know scarcely anyone in London, and I quite long for company."

"You do? Truly? You aren't just doing the polite?"

"Indeed not. In fact, you could do me the greatest service, if you don't mind. You see," she said awkwardly, "Harry had meant to ask a friend to be my escort while he was gone. But I fear it quite slipped his mind. And he's left me the most handsome allowance imaginable for the theater and such. And I cannot tell you how I long to see the plays and visit the opera and—"

"See Astley's Royal Circus?" Mr. Combe chimed in.

"Oh, yes, indeed. And the Elgin Marbles and—"

"And attend Almack's?" Mr. Combe asked hopefully.

"Oh, dear, I fear not. Harry did say he'd approach the Princess Esterhazy for a voucher for me, but either he forgot or she turned him down."

"He forgot then," Mr. Combe pronounced. "The princess wouldn't refuse Harry. But never mind. We shall have enough to keep us occupied."

"Then you will not mind serving as my escort?"

"Mind? I shall like it above all things."

Mr. Combe and Mrs. Romney beamed delightedly at one another.

Chapter
Eleven

IT WAS DECIDED THAT THEY SHOULD ATTEND COVENT Garden that very night. The footman was dispatched for tickets and the evening found them seated in their box, rivaling each other as to who was the more excited.

Evelyn was the ideal escort for Alexandria. Even though, unlike her, he had attended the theater a few times before, his visits to London had been too infrequent to allow him to become jaded. He was looking very handsome, Alexandria thought, somewhat relieved that the prescribed evening clothes he wore allowed him little scope to exercise his sartorial flare.

And she had never been so pleased with her own looks. For the first time she was able to wear one of the new gowns she had purchased, white gauze over a blue satin underdress, the exact color of her eyes, worn daringly low on the bust and shoulders; though not so low as to challenge the squire's daughter's taste. Since she possessed no jewelry, she had made do with a spray of flowers twined skillfully by Maggie into her upswept hair. Satin slippers, kid gloves, and an ivory fan made her feel quite up to snuff. And if, when she first gazed around at the occupants of the other boxes and took due note of all their finery, her confidence in her own appearance slipped substantially, it was almost immediately restored by the look of frank admiration in her young escort's eyes.

They had come early and were enjoying the unsophisticated pastime of quizzing the crowd as the theater filled up. Nor was their enthusiasm dampened all that much when word began to spread that the great Kemble, whom most had come to see and not the play, would not appear. For years Mr. Kemble had been the undisputed ruling monarch of the London stage. But now he was close to retirement and appearing less and less. And there was some talk about a new actor, Edmund Kean of Drury Lane, ready to usurp his crown.

"Never mind," Evelyn said philosophically as news of Kemble's absence swept the theater. "We'll see him another time. Let's just hope they keep the farce."

But if the defection of the celebrated actor could not spoil their enjoyment of the evening, another circumstance almost did. Just before the curtain rose, they were joined by Oliver. He had an immediate dampening effect upon both their spirits, although for different reasons.

As he bowed low over Alexandria's hand, murmuring that he'd never seen her look lovelier, she felt the same longings she had always felt, in spite of her resolutions to put all such feelings in the past. If only he were not quite so handsome!

Mr. Combe had risen, colored, and given Sir Oliver the smallest of awkward bows when he had come striding into their box. After holding Alexandria's hand a bit too long for mere politeness, Oliver then turned toward Evelyn, who went on the defensive.

"Does your stepfather know you're here?" the older man inquired.

Evelyn was on the verge of telling him that it was none of his cursed affair, but checked the hasty words in time. Instead, he replied sulkily that he had only just arrived at Harry's and would call on Lord Woolridge the next day.

"And where is Harry?" It was difficult for Oliver to keep his dislike for his cousin from his voice even in social small talk. The question was more or less addressed to Alexandria but, fortunately for her peace of mind, Evelyn chose to answer.

"Away on business," he said. "And where is your new bride?"

It was Oliver's turn, much to the surprise of the other occupants of the box, to color. "She is at home," he said. "She had to send her regrets at the last moment to Lord and Lady Edgemont. Their party is just across the way there." He nodded to a box on the opposite side of the theater, where half a dozen elegantly dressed people stood in conversation. "Amelia was devastated to have to cry off. Lord Edgemont is a very close associate of her father." Oliver quite failed to disguise his obvious pleasure in his wife's connections.

"Then why did your wife cry off?" If Mr. Combe

recognized the rudeness of the query, he failed to show it.

Again Alexandria was conscious of Oliver's embarrassment. "Amelia is indisposed," he answered reluctantly. "Nothing serious, mind you. She simply is not feeling quite the thing."

And then the truth dawned upon Alexandria. Amelia must be enceinte. It was all she could do not to glare accusingly at Oliver. Such haste to breed seemed in the poorest taste. The ink was barely dry upon their marriage lines. So much for his undying love for her!

Oliver excused himself to find his seat just before the curtain rose. But for Alexandria much of the enjoyment had gone from the evening. It took quite a little time before she was able to lose herself in the melodrama unfolding upon the stage.

But at that she did better than most of her fellow patrons. Seasoned theatergoers, angered by the defection of the principal actor they had come to see, seemed to find his substitute worse than second-rate. The theater was largely filled with members of the ton, so even the patrons in the pit refrained from throwing things. But boos, hisses, and catcalls punctuated most of the speeches from the leading man.

Then suddenly there was a commotion from a third-tier box quite near the stage, occupied mostly by men, Alexandria noted, though the tips of some golden plumage indicated that at least one female was among the group. It would appear that the occupants were deep into their cups. This box had been the source of much of the heckling. Their tolerance of the substitute performer, always tenuous at best, was now at an end.

As the substitute on the stage launched into a quivering rendition of Kemble's famous soliloquy, one member of the noisy group, clutching a bottle in his hand, leaped suddenly upon the box ledge and teetered there precariously, to the encouraging applause of its other occupants.

The effect was electrifying. All eyes, from the gallery to the pit, switched from the stage to the tall young man in the dark coat and white satin breeches who rocked dizzily back and forth upon the ledge. The terrified actor's speech wound down like the ninth day of an eight-day clock and finally faded altogether. The bulk of the audience was similarly stricken. Only the group within the raucous box seemed unmoved by any sense of peril. They were noisily engaged in placing bets upon the ability of the tall man with the bottle to keep his balance.

"Count me in too," the teetering gentleman called out to a well-dressed colleague who was busily covering bets against him. He danced a jig upon the ledge to raise the odds and laughed delightedly as the spectators directly below him became alive to their own imminent disaster and unfroze to scamper to the center of the pit.

"My God, it's Harry!" Evelyn croaked as Alexandria, who had just realized the same thing, clutched at him. Young Combe trained his glass rather unsteadily upon the swaying figure. "It's him, all right. And he's bosky as anything. Why doesn't someone stop him?"

But obviously Harry's comrades had no intention of doing so. All bets now laid, they began to cheer him on. The capacity crowd, with characteristic herd instinct, began to lose its initial fright for the young man's peril and joined in the clamor from the box. The Romans must have acted just this way in the Circus Maximus, Alexandria thought with mounting horror.

"Go, Harry, go!" the occupants of the box chanted, and the gallery took it up. "Go, Harry, go!"

Mr. Romney raised the port bottle in a salute, bowed to the box, then toward the pit, whose occupants gasped in unison as it appeared he would topple over. Harry laughed uproariously at the reaction, then placed one hand upon the separating column and arced far out over the precipice before winding up upon the ledge of the adjoining box. There he stood balancing like a walker upon a rope while its occupants recoiled from him and the gallery cheered. And then a sudden hush fell over the noisy theater as it became evident just what the inebriated young man intended to do. Even his fellow revelers in the box he'd left behind seemed stunned to sobriety.

Afterwards it was said that Astley's Royal Circus had never seen the like of the athletic feat performed by Harry Romney in Covent Garden Theater. With almost careless precision he walked the narrow horseshoe ledge around the boxes while the audience in the pit clustered close together like a herd of cattle buffeted by the wind and shifted noiselessly with frightened, upraised faces from one location to another, trying to avoid being directly underneath him when luck ran out for the drunken, elegant young swell and his body plummeted.

Instinctively Alexandria and Evelyn, still clutching one another, had crept back into the darker recesses of their box as Harry's tightrope walk drew nearer. The last thing they wished to do was to distract him by their presence. But their retreat proved futile. Harry spied them anyhow. And for the first time, perhaps, his wavering on the ledge lost its stagy quality.

"Is that you, Evelyn?" He peered at the two quaking spectators in the shadows.

"Y-y-yes," a strangled voice answered him.

"Well, I say then, unhand my wife!" Harry declaimed loudly in a Kemble voice, then laughed uproariously and swayed backward toward the pit, whose occupants gasped in horror like a practiced chorus.

"Oh, Harry, do come down." Alexandria found her voice and pleaded softly.

"I can't do that. Only halfway round," her husband replied cheerfully. "Wouldn't be sporting to stop now, don't you know. Besides," he added practically, "I'd drop a bundle. By the way, Alex, did I remark that you look smashing?"

Somehow Alexandria wished he had used a different word. "Harry, please," she pleaded. But with an airy wave of the hand he was off once more.

He did, however, increase his pace, as if suddenly bored with the escapade, and sprinted from box to box with the precision of a mountain goat. He arrived quickly above the stage, where he knelt, then hung by his hands from the box ledge, dropped to the tier below, teetered a moment, then proceeded in the same fashion, to the accompaniment of gasps, till he at last plummeted upon the stage in a roar of thunderous applause. It ended finally in a standing ovation by the crowd while he bowed theatrically.

Alexandria and Evelyn did not, however, join in

the tumultuous tribute. Instead, they fell back weakly upon their chairs and stared at one another. The nervous reaction they were suffering left them only dimly aware that Harry was being hoisted up on the shoulders of his cronies and borne in triumph from the theater, or that the curtain had creaked down to rise again shortly while the thespians tried valiantly to pick up the play where they'd left it off. They need not have bothered. The theater was abuzz with talk of the death-defying acrobatic feat. The great Kemble himself could not have held this audience. The Honorable Henry Romney's act was impossible to follow.

Alexandria and Evelyn were just far enough recovered for Mr. Combe to say, "You could have blown me over like a feather when I realized that the cove balanced on the edge was Harry. I don't mind saying I've been so—"

But he was not allowed to finish what he'd planned to say, for at that moment they were joined by a very agitated Oliver.

"Come, Alexandria," he said. "I shall take you home."

"Oh, I say," Evelyn Combe protested. "She's with me. If anybody takes her home, I shall. In fact, it's my home too, temporarily that is, so I'd be going there anyhow. Not that that—"

"Never mind," Oliver snapped. "Hurry, Alexandria."

"Why should she?" Mr. Combe asked belligerently. "There's still more of the play to come and I told you that I'd—"

"You don't seem to understand." Oliver spoke icily. "I'm trying to shield Alexandria from any further embarrassment."

"Why should she be embarrassed? If you mean because Harry did a balcony walk, what does that have to say to her? For that matter, I don't know why even Harry need feel embarrassed. I should think he might have an advanced case of the horrors when he sobers up and realizes he could have broken his neck, but he'll have no need to feel embarrassed. It was a damn fine stunt," Mr. Combe concluded stoutly. "I don't know another single cove who could have done it."

"I don't know another one fool enough to try," Oliver replied. "Alexandria." He turned his back on young Evelyn and appealed to her instead. "I do think you should leave now. The place is rampant with gossip and someone is sure to realize just who you are after Harry singled you out so thoughtlessly. And it's bound to be reported," he added bitterly. "Undoubtedly there'll be one or two newspapermen in the pit right now. It really won't do, you know, to have them badgering you—or you either, for that matter," he said over his shoulder to Evelyn. "Harry's timing was, as usual, reprehensible. Lord Woolridge's bill is due to be presented before the House. The opposition is bound to make political hay of Harry's latest escapade."

"So that's what concerns you." Evelyn sounded scornful.

"Most certainly it is. And I think you, too, might show a bit of concern for Lord Woolridge's interests."

"Come on, Evelyn, please," Alexandria whispered. With undisguised reluctance, Evelyn helped her on with her cloak and they followed Oliver out into the street. Alexandria had expected him to speed them on their way once he'd whistled up some loitering chairmen for them. Instead, much to Evelyn's disgust, he insisted upon accompanying them to Grosvenor Square. And once ensconced inside drinking the tea Alexandria had ordered for them, his first business of the evening was to read young Mr. Combe a lecture.

"I do think you should have let your father know your whereabouts," he said severely, as if Evelyn were seven instead of seventeen. "If I am not mistaken, he has made it quite clear in the past that he prefers you stay under his roof instead of Harry's while you're in town. You know he does not consider his son the proper influence for a young man of your tender years."

"Harry was not even here," Evelyn replied sulkily.

"That's even worse, then."

"Are you implying that my wife is more likely to lead the stripling from the paths of virtue than I am? Come now, Oliver. Granted you probably know Alex a great deal better than I do, but isn't that a bit strong?"

None of them had heard Harry enter. He stood in the door, looking none the worse for his adventure, Alexandria noted. His evening clothes became him, she thought inconsequentially as she noted the muscles of his calves under the white silk hose. His bearing was actually better than Oliver's. It came from being an athlete, she supposed. She jerked her thoughts back to the matters of the moment and looked at him warily, wondering just how deep into his cups he was.

He seemed to read her mind, for he smiled sardonically. "Checking me for signs of dissipation, are you, Mrs. Romney?"

128

"Don't be absurd," she answered a bit too heart-ily. "Would you care for some tea?"

"Why not?" He strolled into the room and took a chair, stretching out upon it languidly. "This is a cozy family gathering. Like Cousin Oliver, I'm sur-prised to find you here, Evelyn. Deuced pleased, of course." A grin lightened his harsh countenance for a moment. "But still surprised. Been here long?" He helped himself to some seed cake and took a bite large enough to cause Oliver to flinch.

"No, I only just arrived, and I say, Harry—"

"And you, Oliver," his host interrupted. His voice was pleasantly conversational through the mouth-ful of cake, but there was no corresponding softness of expression. "I never used to find you in my par-lor in the past. But then conditions here have changed. As you doubtless are aware, I'm seldom here myself. I fear Alexandria has been left very much alone. Is that, perhaps, why you object to Evelyn's presence?"

"This is the first time I've been in your house since your marriage." Oliver's voice shook with rage. "How dare you imply—"

"Really?" Harry's eyebrows rose as if in disbelief. Then he shrugged. "Perhaps it's true. You always were a slowtop."

"Stop it, Harry." Alexandria spoke severely, for-getting completely her resolution not to interfere no matter how outrageously he behaved. "Can you never be in Oliver's presence for five minutes with-out seeking to get a rise from him?"

"Never mind," Oliver growled. "It's quite obvious what he is doing."

"It is? What is that?" Harry inquired.

"Trying to throw up a smokescreen to take the

attention away from your own scandalous behavior. I suppose you know that you have become the *on-dit* of London."

"No, I did not know it. But I suppose you're going to tell me."

"Someone should," Oliver retorted bitterly. "If you have no regard for the sensibilities of your wife—"

"Regard?" Harry interrupted. "I never knew she had 'em. Alex, did I wound your sensibilities?"

"Stop acting like a schoolboy," his wife replied, trying to sound severe but stifling a giggle that produced a kindred spark of amusement in her husband's eyes.

"But I don't have that much choice," he protested pleasantly, "if Oliver insists on playing headmaster and dragging me on the carpet for my sins. Come to think of it, Oliver, you would have made an excellent schoolmaster. How you would have enjoyed caning the little beggars on their backsides."

Evelyn snorted in appreciation, incurring a quelling glance from Oliver. "Perhaps if you had had more of that sort of thing as a schoolboy it might have made you more aware of your position."

"I did have and I was. Across the desk with my britches dropped—that was my commonest position."

"There's no possibility of having a serious discussion with you, I see." Oliver placed his cup and saucer carefully on the sofa table and rose to his feet. "You are obviously not prepared to admit that tonight's disgraceful behavior will cause your father a great deal of embarrassment and injure him politically."

"Oh, I say, that's not fair," Evelyn interposed.

Harry had stood too. "If the fate of the nation must rise or fall because I walked around the Covent Garden horseshoe on the box ledges, then I fear that the empire is doomed indeed."

"He's right you know, Oliver. What he does has nothing to say to—"

"Has it not?" Oliver turned to glare at Evelyn. "If you are no naïve as not to know that bringing down ridicule upon a political opponent's head is the surest way to scotch his serious purposes, well, I assure you, Harry is not."

"Are you implying, cousin"— Harry's dark eyes narrowed—"that I did my balcony walk deliberately in order to defeat my father's bill?"

"Perhaps not deliberately," Oliver qualified, whether from an awakened sense of fairness or from the sudden dangerous demeanor of his cousin, Alexandria could not decide. "But it is certainly true that you have never been known to show the slightest consideration for his feelings or his position. And now it would seem that you are prepared to treat your wife with equal carelessness."

"I think that will do, cousin. I think you have just overstepped your bounds. Perhaps there is some justice in your attack on my filial shortcomings. But I do not think Alexandria would agree that she's been treated shabbily."

This time Oliver chose to ignore the menace in Harry's voice. "Alexandria is by nature an uncomplaining sort. What other wife would be so tolerant of seeing her husband at the theater with his mistress?"

Involuntarily, Alexandria gasped. For the first time she recalled the plumes she'd seen among the heads of the inebriated gentlemen in Harry's box.

"We didn't see any mistress," Evelyn interposed angrily, "but you've taken care to make her presence known, I see."

"Never mind." Harry placed a restraining hand on Evelyn's sleeve. "It is good of you, Oliver, to be so concerned for Alexandria's feelings. But would you not be better occupied with Amelia's sensibilities? I cannot think she will be too pleased, considering your past history of devotion to Alexandria, to hear of your dramatic exit from Covent Garden with my wife. She could consider it a case of oversolicitousness on your part. Ladies in her delicate condition are not noted for their rational outlook, I understand."

"How dare you imply—" Oliver's voice was choked with rage as he took a threatening step toward Harry. "Retract your insinuations immediately," he sputtered, but Harry merely folded his arms across his chest and gazed at him with interest. Oliver took one more threatening step. "You really are a bastard," he said between clenched teeth.

Harry's arms unfolded with lightning speed and, before Oliver saw, much less tried to feint, the blow, an iron fist uppercut his chin and he found himself stretched out upon the floor. "I don't mind a bit of gentlemanly name-calling," Harry remarked almost casually, "but bastard is not a word that I permit."

"Harry, you beast!" Alexandria screeched and rushed in Oliver's direction. Harry, however, seemed to think that he should be the object of his wife's attention, for he grabbed her and held her fast.

"I'm warning you now, Alex, if you so much as

say a word in that clodpole's defense, I'll not be responsible."

"You big bully, you could have killed him! He's no boxer and you know it," Alexandria fumed. "Let me go!" She punctuated her request by a swift kick at Harry's shins.

"Ow! Damn it all, that did it!" Mr. Romney tightened his grip on Mrs. Romney and pulled her hard against his chest. Then, because he seemed at a total loss as to what to do now that he had her pinned, he reached down and none too gently tilted up her chin, then planted his mouth roughly upon her lips.

Later, when she tried to sort the whole thing out, she recalled that Harry's kiss had not been exactly nice—at least, compared to the almost chaste caresses she had known from Oliver—and she did not doubt that he had spent far too much time in the company of Cyprians. But at the moment she was conscious of a buzzing in her ears and of feeling rather faint, a curious state of affairs that she blamed entirely upon the excitement of the evening. She was forced to cling rather limply to Harry's muscular frame.

When he finally released her, Harry looked almost apologetic. "Damn it all, Alex, you really don't give a fellow a lot of choice. After all, when you went on the attack, I could hardly deliver you a facer."

For a moment she simply stared at him wide-eyed. "Oliver!" she then gasped, suddenly recalling her injured cousin. "Oh, do ring for Padgett." She gave her husband, who still held her in his arms, a hard push toward the bell rope and ran to kneel over the prone Oliver. Harry stood gazing for a moment at the tableau, his face a mask, before he slowly moved to obey her order.

Alexandria was helping Oliver to sit up when the butler entered and took in the scene with no more apparent interest than he would have shown if the company were engaged in a game of whist.

"Padgett, do bring us some cold compresses for Sir Oliver. He has just fallen," she improvised, as Mr. Evelyn Combe snorted and Harry grinned a crooked grin. "And some laudanum, if you please. Does it hurt terribly?" she inquired solicitously as the butler left to do her bidding. Oliver's only answer was a groan.

"I think he'll recover," Harry remarked. "Well, now, having made myself even more popular with my family, I'll take my leave. Evelyn, would you like to accompany me? I think we can safely leave Oliver to the ministrations of my wife. She does seem to enjoy being his nursemaid."

"Why, yes, of course I'd like to come with you." Evelyn's eyes sparkled with enthusiasm. "Just let me get my things."

"You know that your father will not approve," Oliver said thickly, holding his throbbing head between his hands. "Where are you taking him?" The last remark was addressed to Harry.

"Why, to Harriette Wilson's. Where else?"

"My God!" Oliver raised his head too quickly and groaned from the ensuing pain. "You actually intend to take a seventeen-year-old youth to that— that—"

"Bordello?" Harry helpfully supplied.

"I would have spared Alexandria the term, but yes, since you insist. Do you really intend to take your brother-in-law, a mere schoolboy, to a brothel?"

"I really think Harriette would prefer the term bordello. It sounds better. Her clients are unexceptional, you know."

"I won't be a moment." Young Evelyn fairly danced out of the room before Harry could be dissuaded from including him in the evening's program.

"I can assure you I shall not hesitate to report this whole shameful affair to Lord Woolridge."

"I rather thought you might, Oliver."

Padgett arrived with a basin and some cloths upon a tray, along with an apothecary's bottle. Alexandria picked up the laudanum and poured a generous amount into a spoon.

"For goodness sake, Oliver," she said crossly, "can't you see that Harry hasn't the slightest intention of taking Evelyn to a place like that, no matter what you both decide to call it? It's just one more of his rather childish attempts to get you in a taking. Is it not, Harry?"

She glared at her husband accusingly. He merely shrugged.

"Come now, why can't you admit that you have no intention of getting Evelyn into any kind of scrape? Really, Harry, have you not caused enough mischief for one evening?"

Harry watched in silence for a moment as Alexandria spooned the dose of laudanum into Oliver's mouth and applied a cool cloth tenderly to his swelling jaw.

"Yes, it would appear I have," he answered at last. He turned abruptly and left the room.

Chapter Twelve

AFTER THE COVENT GARDEN THEATER INCIDENT, Alexandria's life turned another corner. The initial phase left her quite dejected, for the next morning Evelyn disclosed his intention of removing at once to Brook Street.

"Must you?" she blurted out without thinking. Evelyn's exuberant presence had seemed a godsend. She had looked forward to some delightful excursions about London.

"It won't change things that much," he reassured her. "We can still go about together, that is if you ain't finding me a nuisance by now." He colored with pleasure at her quick denial. "But Harry felt it would be a good thing all around if I used my stepfather's house as my headquarters. As he said, I can still spend as much time with you as you'll put up with. I thought it rather a good idea, for Harry's sake, don't you know. In order to keep his father from holding one more thing against him. He had absolutely nothing to do with my coming here, of course, but that snake Oliver will make it appear that he's leading me astray."

"Evelyn, you have no right to be so critical of Oliver." Alexandria leaped automatically to the defense. "After all, if Harry persists in telling such Banbury Tales, what can he expect? Harriette Wilson's establishment, indeed!" She sniffed.

Evelyn grinned at the recollection. "If Oliver were not such a widgeon, he'd know that Harry was merely roasting him."

"Oliver is unaccustomed to Harry's particular brand of humor," she said severely. "By the by, where *did* you go? Or am I allowed to ask?"

"You can ask, all right," he answered glumly as she accompanied him outside. "Pity that Harry was just roasting Oliver, for I'd give a monkey to see the inside of Harriette's establishment. Now, don't start reading me a lecture, for I ain't likely to. Not for a few years, at any rate. But, to answer your question, we went to Watier's."

"Watier's! Lord Woolridge will consider that a step up from Harriette's, I suppose, but only a very slight one."

"He'd be wasting his time flying up into the boughs over it, I'll tell you, for Harry would not allow me to sit in. Said they played too deep. As if I could not handle myself!" He sounded very young and very aggrieved.

Alexandria laughed at his long face and saw him into his carriage. "You'll just have to postpone gambling at Watier's for a few years, along with Harriette Wilson. Evelyn, I can see that you've quite a dissolute future ahead of you."

"Oh, Alex—" Evelyn had adopted Harry's form of address for her and, though Alexandria sighed inwardly for it, she did not try to correct the habit. "I almost forgot." He leaned out of the carriage that would transport him and his luggage to Brook Street. "Harry said he was sorry about Almack's. It slipped his mind. He plans to attend to it right away, though. Promise you'll let me take you there."

"I promise." She smiled as he drove away.

There was no time for Alexandria to become blue-deviled after she had waved goodbye. Evelyn's departure was soon followed by an early morning visitor. Maggie, her maid, burst into Alexandria's room and announced, "Lord Woolridge is here, ma'am. Asking for Mr. Romney. Padgett thought it best that you should speak to him."

"Oh, dear." Alexandria looked at Maggie in consternation. "Yes, I suppose I should. Does he appear—uh—out of sorts?" There was no need to pretend with Maggie. Alexandria knew that, by now, the servants would know every detail of the previous evening's scandal.

"I wouldn't say out of sorts exactly, ma'am. I'd say he looked more stony-like."

"Oh, dear." Alexandria sighed once more, glanced in the glass to give her hair a smoothing pat, and went downstairs to greet her husband's father.

She was not encouraged to find Lord Woolridge striding back and forth like a caged lion in the small parlor. "I had hoped to see my son," was his initial abrupt response to her "Good morning." Perhaps she only imagined that he gave the word "son" an ironic twist. "Since Padgett has been, to say the least, evasive on the subject, I hope you will be more forthcoming. Am I to take it, then, that he is not here?"

"No, sir," Alexandria replied nervously. "I mean to say, yes, sir." She took a deep breath and tried again. "I meant to say that, yes, you are right. Harry is not here."

He had stopped his pacing when she entered. Now he fixed her with a level stare. "And would I also be right in assuming that he is not in residence here, and that your marriage is a sham?"

Her face flamed red. "No, he is not staying here at the moment. But you mistake the other matter. We most certainly are wed."

"In the legal sense, you mean," Lord Woolridge replied brutally. "But in actuality Harry is living with his mistress, as before."

"I-I do not know," she stammered.

"Oh, do you not?" For the first time Lord Woolridge's face reflected the bitterness he was feeling. "Young lady, please do not dissemble with me. I find it extremely difficult to believe you have not been in collusion with my son from the very first."

"Collusion? I'm sure I don't know what you mean."

"I think you do. I think you knowingly entered into a sham marriage with my son. And I think his only motive was to strike back at me because I had requested that he marry and settle down. In a word, to change his way of life for the sake of his family's reputation. He must consider this letter of the law obedience an immense joke. Really, it quite eclipses last night's feat." He gave a low laugh that was chilling in its lack of humor.

Alexandria looked at him in some distress. For the first time it occurred to her that it was not just Lord Woolridge's political career that was at issue. Harry's conduct had cut deeper into his pride than that. "I really believe you are mistaken," she began, talking partly to herself, then held up a hand to stop Woolridge's contradiction. "I don't mean about our marriage being a pretense. And my being in collusion, as you call it. For Harry did lay all his cards upon the table and tell me that he wanted me to be his wife only in a legal way." Alexandria grew more and more embarrassed under Woolridge's piercing stare. She wished he did not remind her quite so much of an older, sterner Oliver.

She stumbled on. "Where I think you are in error, sir, is in the motives you ascribe to Harry. I think he really did want to please you. I think he went north seriously intending to offer for Lady Amelia's sister, but then he funked it." She paused a moment to look at Lord Woolridge accusingly. "Have you ever met Lady Arabel Fielding?"

"No. However—" Lord Woolridge began, but she interrupted rudely.

"I thought not. Have you ever seen Harry's mistress?"

"I have not had that pleasure either," he answered dryly.

"If you had, you might understand, for she is most beautiful. But even if she were not—or did not exist, for that matter—it was the sheerest folly to expect Harry to marry Arabel Fielding. She really is a most insipid female. Not at all in Harry's style."

"Whereas you—" Lord Woolridge's voice was laced with heavy sarcasm.

She felt her cheeks turn red. "My case was very different. Harry saw the opportunity to comply with your wishes without actually . . ."

She tried to find a delicate way to phrase her thought, but Lord Woolridge saved her the necessity. "Without inconveniencing himself at all."

"Well, yes," she admitted. "Also, he was rescuing me from a most intolerable situation."

"How gallant."

"It was, rather." She was more than a little nettled by his tone. "And I'm grateful for it. And though I see now it was shatter-brained of him to think so, I do think he felt he was acting in your best interests as well."

"I must say that Henry has purchased himself a loyal wife." His father sneered while Alexandria tried to check her rising anger. "Now, tell me. Was last night's exhibition also in my interests?"

"No, it was not," she answered him steadily. "I think he was simply intoxicated past all sense and acted upon impulse, egged on by his companions. It had nothing to do with you. And there's no doubt, of course," she added, in a sense of fairness, "that there's a very regrettable streak of wildness to be found in Harry."

"Streak is an understatement," Harry's father replied. "Wildness is a commodity that the Flynns, his mother's people, have always possessed in abundance. Not unusual with the Irish, I collect."

"No doubt you're right. But there's another quality I've come to perceive in Harry that appears to me to be all Romney. At least it's a trait both of you seem to have in common." Alexandria realized that she would win no prizes for her tact, but she found herself desperately wanting to humanize Lord

Woolridge. His expression, however, was not encouraging. He had reverted to his previous stoniness.

"I think you are mistaken. Henry and I share nothing in common."

"Forgive me for disagreeing, but perhaps it takes a newcomer to recognize it. For I would definitely say that you both have the same excess of pride."

"If we do both possess that trait, which I'm not prepared to admit in Henry's case," Lord Woolridge said, reaching for the hat, cane, and gloves he'd deposited upon a table, "it certainly manifests itself in different ways. No, I fear that my son and I are as different as two men can be."

"You certainly are not the first man to think so." Alexandria tried to inject a lighter tone into the conversation. "Take the King, for instance. He must think at times that all seven of his sons are changelings." She stopped, appalled at what she had just said. She prayed that the floor might open up and swallow her.

Lord Woolridge, however, merely raised his eyebrows. "No, I doubt His Majesty seriously considers illegitimacy a possibility, no matter how greatly he must at times have wished for it. So he and I do not really make that good a parallel."

"I did not mean—" Alexandria choked.

"Oh, did you not? Come now, Alexandria. You could not have stayed in Lady Augusta's company as long as you did without hearing the rumors of your husband's parentage."

"Lady Augusta is a spiteful gossip monger. No right-thinking adult would pay the slightest bit of attention to that kind of talk. But the problem is— and, mind you, this is the merest speculation on my part—I think Harry must have heard the stories when he was still young enough to be hurt by them. You know what children are like. At any rate, it was when Oliver called him that word—bastard, I mean"—she colored at the repetition of such vulgarity—"that Harry knocked him down."

"Oliver called Henry a bastard?" For the first time, Lord Woolridge actually looked shocked.

"Oliver did have considerable provocation," Alexandria hastened to explain.

"Of that I have little doubt."

"But the point I was hoping to make was this. It could be that Harry has been damaged more than you realize by the gossip. Perhaps you should talk to him."

"Why should I do that?" Lord Woolridge bent a frosty look upon her. "Indeed, I cannot discover how it is that you and I are having this unseemly conversation, and I've certainly no intention of opening up the distasteful subject with Henry."

"But don't you see? The point is that as a child Harry would not have been able to discount the gossip for what it was—malicious tittle-tattle. And he'd be left with impressions and attitudes that he'd not even question in his adult years. I really think you owe it to him to set the record straight."

"To tell him that he is not illegitimate? I should find that rather difficult," Lord Woolridge said.

"I beg your pardon?"

"You heard me correctly."

"Are you telling me it's true?" She stared at him, appalled as much by his icy calm as by his words.

"No, certainly not." He drew on his gloves. "After all, what man can be sure of the parentage of his child? But if you ask me what is most probable, I

143

should say it's that Harry is not mine. Don't look so shocked. This is not mere cynicism on my part. You see, I had the information from a rather more reliable source than Lady Augusta Linnell."

"You did?" Her voice was little better than a whisper. "Who would have been cruel enough to tell you that?"

"The person most likely to know the truth. Henry's mother."

Lord Woolridge smiled bitterly at Alexandria, then bowed politely and left her standing there. She remained rooted to the spot long after the echo of his footsteps had died away.

Chapter Thirteen

THE SECOND VISITOR OF HER DAY FOLLOWED TOO RAP-
idly on the first for Alexandria to do more
than thrust her bizarre conversation with Lord
Woolridge to the back of her mind.

Even Padgett lost a bit of his aplomb and allowed
his eyes to reach the popping stage when he announced, "The Countess de Lieven to see you,
ma'am."

The Countess de Lieven was the wife of the am-
bassador from Russia. She was intelligent and attractive, and had managed to enter the *crème de la
crème* of English society. She had charmed the Regent, it was said, and counted among her intimates
the great political figures of the day—Castlereagh,
Canning, the Duke of Wellington, Lord Grey. It was
also whispered, mainly among the wives of the various males she wrapped around her little finger,

that no state secret was safe from her. But, most of all, she was a patroness of Almack's.

These patronesses were the guardians of the gates of that exclusive social club, and they ruled it despotically. The Ladies Castlereagh, Jersey, and Cowper, the Princess Esterhazy, and the Countess de Lieven held the power of social life and death in their aristocratic hands. For it was they who decided who should and who should not receive voucher invitations.

In a way, perhaps Lord Woolridge's upsetting visit worked to Alexandria's advantage. For when the countess was announced, she was too concerned with more important matters to be put into a quake over a visit clearly designed to look her over. She concentrated instead upon not betraying to the countess the fact that her morning call had been badly timed.

This proved easier than she might have hoped for. Although the Countess de Lieven was considered by most to be entirely too high in the instep for a Russian and dauntingly exclusive, it soon became apparent that she was consumed by curiosity.

She made it quite clear as tea was being served that her "dear, dear Harry" had requested that she call upon his bride. "How like the naughty Harry to sweep you away in an elopement! And how romantic! Most un-English, really. But then, Harry is always the exception."

The half-smile on the rather sensuous lips and the first glimpse of animation in the handsome, haughty face caused Alexandria to wonder suddenly just how dear "dear, dear Harry" was. Rumors abounded about the countess's many lovers, though it was said she never seriously involved

146

herself with any man, a state of affairs likely to have a great appeal for Harry. Alexandria looked at her guest curiously, but the face had resumed its diplomatic mask.

It soon became evident, however, that, although the countess was indeed making a duty call at the Honorable Henry Romney's express request, the timing of the visit was all her own idea. Word had reached her of the Covent Garden episode and she was desirous to learn all she could about it. It would give her something new to talk of for a week, perhaps.

Alexandria, though admitting she'd been present at the theater, was reluctant to discuss the incident. But, little by little, she found the tale being skillfully drawn out of her. "No, indeed, Harry was not foxed past all repair. He could not have managed so dangerous an acrobatic feat if he had been raddled as all that." And, "No, indeed, he did not make his mistress known to me." She began to see why it was that the Russian countess was considered a danger as far as state matters were concerned. She certainly was adept at finding out whatever she desired to know without ever appearing to pump the object of her interrogation.

But when she steered the conversation around to the reaction of Lord Woolridge, whom she had noted leaving the house as she'd arrived, Alexandria saw no reason not to be quite candid. "He was not pleased, of course. People in political life live in glass houses. And Harry's escapade could not have been more badly timed as far as he's concerned."

"You refer to Lord Woolridge's bill? I fail to see—" The countess shrugged delicately.

"So do I. But I think Lord Woolridge fears that his serious purposes will now be subject to ridicule."

"But that's absurd," the countess replied, wrinkling her slightly overlong, aristocratic nose. "I think, if anything, Harry has helped, not hurt, Woolridge's career. Harry is quite popular, you know."

"No, I did not," Alexandria blurted, then colored under the countess's knowing stare.

"Oh, yes, indeed. He has enemies and detractors, of course. Who has not? But he is greatly admired by many for his elan and his dash. Lord Woolridge, on the other hand, in spite of being so very handsome and distinguished looking, is quite a dull, dry stick."

Something in the lady's tone left Alexandria wondering if perhaps Woolridge was one intended victim who had resisted the Russian's flirts. She quickly abandoned the idea as quite absurd.

"If his bill does not make it through the house," the countess continued, "it will be due to his lack of leadership and not his son's wild starts."

The countess rose to her feet at the end of the prescribed fifteen mintues for social calls. As Alexandria escorted her to the door, the Countess de Lieven assured her with a charming smile that she would be receiving a voucher card for the Assemblies and that her most delightful brother-in-law would be welcome also. Alexandria thanked her prettily, she hoped, though at the moment she did not feel capable of all the raptures that the Almack patroness's condescension called for. But she would be pleased eventually, she knew. And Evelyn, she was sure, would be ecstatic enough for both of them.

It was as though the countess had opened up the floodgates. As the word spread of her morning call,

Alexandria was beset by a rush of visitors. All the *haut ton* seemed most anxious to meet the new Mrs. Romney, and, if they were propelled to Grosvenor Square as much by curiosity as by courtesy—for the word had also been spread, Alexandria realized, about the Romneys' singular living style—she was growing worldly-wise enough to overlook it. The contrast to her first days of loneliness in the metropolis was quite pronounced, and time flew by in a flurry of visits paid and returned. Cards of invitation to a wide variety of social entertainments were delivered to the door.

But when there was sufficient pause in all the activity to allow time to draw a breath, Alexandria was conscious of a strange and unaccountable *ennui*. In point of fact, she was quite blue-deviled. And a more unreasonable reaction to her present circumstance she could not imagine.

When she dealt honestly with herself, she admitted that her dejection was at its worst when she thought of Oliver. She had not spoken to him privately since the theater debacle, but she had had occasional glimpses of him at some of the social crushes they had both attended.

She and Amelia, however, encountered one another rather frequently on their round of morning calls. While Lady Linnell's interesting condition was not exactly showing, it could be deduced from the new maternal glow upon her face and from the look of triumph mixed with pity that she gave Alexandria when they chanced to meet. It was lowering to realize that, while her own marriage was a pretense, Oliver's was flourishing; that he and his wedded wife were on the most intimate of terms, while she and her husband remained virtual strangers.

Not that she regretted Harry's absence in any way, of course. Indeed, she was grateful for it, just as she was relieved to learn that Lord Woolridge's bill had passed. At least Harry's father could not add its failure to his son's ever-growing list of sins.

And she was grateful that Harry's life had returned to normal. At least, she supposed it had. For when she spoke of him to Evelyn, who was in his company frequently, she was assured that he was "famous, top-of-the-trees." This was reassuring news, of course, but it did not lift her spirits as it should have done.

The problem was, it was impossible for Alexandria to think of Harry without recalling his angry kiss. And, just as inevitably, the memory brought with it burning cheeks and a worrisome confusion. For she had never before been kissed so thoroughly and in such a manner.

She did not refine too much upon the incident, of course. It had simply been the unfortunate culmination of Harry's rage. Since he could not mill her down as he had done Oliver, he'd simply kissed her. What was not so simple was why she had cooperated quite so fully.

She told herself that her reasons were similar to Harry's. Her reaction, too, had been merely the culmination of all the stresses of the evening—her terror for Harry in the theater, her pain at seeing Oliver, her anger at her husband for striking him. And so, finally, Alexandria resolved to think no more about the kiss, a resolution that she discovered was a great deal easier to make than it was to keep in those melancholy, quiet times when she found herself alone.

Chapter Fourteen

L ONDON HAD FALLEN INTO THE GRIP OF A GREAT FROST.
There had been nothing like it, people said,
since the days of Queen Elizabeth. By February the
Thames was frozen solid between London Bridge
and Blackfriars and there were signs everywhere
assuring the public that it was safe to cross. Indeed, a new "Freezeland Street" now stretched
across the river.

Instead of being driven to despair by this severe
weather crisis, the Londoners reacted to it with
amazing cheerfulness and lively imagination. "Oh, I
say, Alex!" Evelyn Combe burst into the Romney
house on Grosvenor Square and shouted up the
stairs. "The most marvelous thing! We mustn't miss
it. Get your things and come along. Mind you bundle
up, though. The tail of a brass monkey wouldn't
stand much chance outside, let alone your ears."

"What on earth are you whooping about?" Mrs. Romney appeared at the head of the stairs and glared down in mock reproach.

"A Frost Fair, that's what!" Evelyn exulted. "It's simply famous! They've set up a fair all along the river. Damnedest thing imaginable. They say they got the idea from Elizabethan days. It was the last time—the first, too, as far as I can tell—that anything like this has happened. Can't you just imagine old Will Shakespeare and Walter Raleigh and all those coves slipping and sliding across on the ice? Come on, Alex. We don't want to miss it."

"Don't get into such a taking. I doubt from what you're telling me that the Thames will melt before we get there."

But all the same, his excitement was infectious. She hurried to put on her new royal blue ermine-lined pelisse and her jaunty cap of matching fur. Stout boots took the place of thin kid slippers. Then, after racing halfway down the stairs and back again to snatch up her white fur muff, she joined the impatient Evelyn in the hall and declared herself ready to brave the bitter cold outside.

"I'll say this for you, Alex." He looked her up and down approvingly. "You don't keep a cove standing about for ages like some females do."

"Are you saying I should spend more time on my appearance?"

"Good lord, no. I ain't saying anything of the kind. There's not a thing wrong with *your* appearance." Evelyn colored and she grinned mischievously.

The city was *en fête*. It seemed that most of the London population had left their heated houses for the icy out-of-doors. Alexandria could not help looking down nervously as they joined the crowds streaming across the river. But soon she was able to forget that somewhere far beneath so many feet, lined by the booths, the swings, the book stalls, the skittle alleys, the printing presses, there underneath the disguising layer of thick ice, the waters of the Thames still sought the sea.

"I say, isn't this famous!" Evelyn crowed for the hundreth time as they jostled with the crowds in order to watch a juggler's frozen fingers protruding from his snipped-off gloves managing somehow to keep an incredible number of small balls whirling in the air. They stood spellbound for a moment, then moved on, shortly to pause again and watch two small, excited children make their selection from the wares of a temporary toy shop.

"Oh, I say, isn't that Harry?" Evelyn whooped joyously. Then a look of consternation replaced his jubilant expression. "No, I was mistaken," he said, quickly taking Alexandria's arm and turning her in quite the opposite direction from the way he'd been looking. She refused, however, to be led, and stared over her shoulder in the direction of his former gaze.

"Indeed, you were not mistaken," she corrected him. "That *is* Harry. Come on." And she gave Evelyn a tug.

"No!" Evelyn yelped and stopped her short. "I don't think we should—ah—bother him just now."

"Why?" she asked, twinkling up at his embarrassed face. "Why should we avoid him just because he has Miss Brady with him?" Alexandria had previously managed to worm the name of Harry's light-of-love from the reluctant Evelyn. "I assure you, he won't mind at all. At least he will not mind if you contrive not to look so Friday-faced."

Evelyn's instinct, however, proved truer in this case than hers. For Harry obviously did mind being hailed and stopped by his stepbrother and his wife as he and his mistress made their leisurely way from one point of interest in the Frost Fair to another.

Nor was Harry the only one who objected to the meeting. After he had made his grudging introductions, the beauty with him looked down her perfect nose at Alexandria and then remarked in a haughty voice only slightly tinged with cockney, "I see that you are wearing your own clothes now, Mrs. Romney. I must say they suit you better than the borrowed ones."

"Yes, do they not?" Alexandria's tone remained unruffled. "Indeed, green is a very poor choice for me. But that is how I recognized you at the emporium. I had guessed that the walking dress I wore was made for someone of your coloring. And now I see that green is a favorite with you." She nodded at the moss-colored fur-lined cloak the beauty wore. "It is most becoming."

"Thank you." Miss Brady's look was frostier than the frozen Thames. "Harry bought this when I refused to wear—"

"Would you excuse us for a moment?" the Honorable Henry broke in rudely. He had obviously had too much of this conversation. "I must speak to Mrs. Romney. Better still, Evelyn, go and show Gwen the fair." And, pressing some money into the delighted young man's hand, he took Alexandria none too gently by the elbow and dragged her away, ignoring Miss Brady's gasp of protest.

"Goodness!" Alexandria slipped on the ice and snatched at Harry to keep from falling. "Do slow down. Why are you in such a taking? And what did you wish to tell me that is so urgent it couldn't wait?"

"The thing I wished to tell you—ask you," Harry snapped, "is, are you blind to all sense of propriety? There are any number of people here who know us and would greatly enjoy seeing the cozy little gathering you just arranged."

She looked up at him in some astonishment. Then she giggled. "Could I have heard you correctly? Is this truly Harry Romney speaking? I could swear you must be Oliver in disguise."

His glare turned to a reluctant grin. *"Touché,"* he said. "But give me some credit, please. I was only thinking of your reputation. I'm accustomed to being the *on-dit* of the town. But I do not think a good deal of gossip would be comfortable for you in your position."

"Fustian. If you do not know that our situation is already grist for the gossip mills, you don't have nearly the town bronze you're supposed to have." They were walking slowly down the rows of tented stalls that lined the river's edge.

"Of course I know that we're talked about. But so far the discredit is all for me."

"Perhaps," she answered doubtfully. "But, in any case, you are right. I should have thought of the impropriety of joining you. What I did think of, actually, was keeping my bargain about not being shrewish over how you live your life. I'm quite determined not to fly up into the boughs over your mistresses or your gambling or your public exhibitions. In short, I mean to be the perfect wife." He glared at

155

her dangerously and she laughed back at him. "And so I thought I was being most broadminded and quite cordial."

"Did you indeed?" he said nastily.

"Oh, yes, I did. But what I failed to take into account was that your—uh—"

"Lady-bird? Light-skirt? Cyprian? Fashionable impure?"

"Your friend might not be so broadminded as I am. She really was in a temper, was she not?"

"You noticed that then, did you? I would have predicted that at any moment she would have had your hair out by the roots." Mrs. Romney looked definitely alarmed and Mr. Romney laughed.

"Surely not!" Alexandria protested.

"There's nothing surely about it," her husband replied. "In spite of the veneer, the fact remains that Gwen Brady is from the Covent Garden area, where they tend to become rather primitive rather fast."

"I think you are roasting me. Surely she could not be in such a pucker over a mere dress."

"I don't think her jealousy is confined to that."

"Jealous? Of me?" Alexandria looked up at him in astonishment. "But that's absurd! She's by far the most beautiful female I have ever seen."

"That's what she said of you."

"She could not have!"

"Perhaps not in just those words," Harry qualified. "But after she'd seen you at Layton & Shear's—which, by the way, was cursed bad luck—she hurled it in my teeth that I'd married a nonpareil instead of some mousy miss from the country as I'd led her to believe."

"You called me that?" Alexandria glared.

"Well." Harry shrugged and grinned. "Gwen said I did. I can't recall what words I used. I expect I was trying to be tactful."

"If so, it was the first time," she retorted. "I'm sorry if I've gotten you into another coil."

"Hypocrite. You wouldn't mind in the least. But the truth is, your little *tête-à-tête* back there has made no difference. Miss Brady and I had already come to the parting of our ways. We were simply trying to work out some of the details. Or, to be exact"— his expression hardened—"Gwen was trying to see how much more besides the house, the carriage, and her clothes and jewelry she could wring out of me."

"You mean she's leaving? How awful for you."

Harry stopped in his tracks. His glare should have melted the ice right out from under Alexandria. "Interesting that you should have put it in just that way."

"Oh, my, I have said entirely the wrong thing, have I not? It's just that she's so beautiful, almost beyond belief."

"Beyond belief that after a certain point I should find her an avaricious, deadly bore? But then you put quite a high premium upon good looks, do you not? At least I could never suppose that Oliver had much to recommend him beyond his quite remarkable surface handsomeness."

The conversation was definitely out of hand. Alexandria, remembering her vow to keep her temper, tried to change its course. "Should we not look for Evelyn and Miss Brady? So you can—uh—finalize your—er—arrangements?"

"Oh, she and I are finished," he answered with no more concern than if he were speaking of the weather. "And I doubt we could find them. I slipped Evelyn ten pounds."

"Goodness, no wonder he was looking dazzled." She laughed gaily, then looked up at Harry in some alarm. "You don't suppose? You did say that Miss Brady is at loose ends. Oh, my goodness! Evelyn has just turned seventeen!"

"Don't worry. Gwen will doubtless be flattered by his moon-calf adulation and his pedigree and she'll certainly enjoy seeing the fair with him, but she's not going to lead him astray, if that's what you're thinking. Penniless halflings are not in her style. Besides, she has my successor lined up already; a wealthy cit"— his lips curled scornfully—"who owns a factory. Who knows? He could be sapskulled enough to marry her. But for God's sake, let's change the subject. I'd had enough of that one before you and Evelyn cornered us. And, by the by, since you aren't likely to see your escort again, shall I take you home?"

"Indeed not! I came to see the fair. And I'll not be fobbed off. This hasn't happened for two hundred years and may not for another two hundred."

"True. By which time you could be quite an old lady. Come on, then. I only wish I could wear that muff you're sporting on my nose." He inched the long woolen scarf he wore up a bit higher toward his ears.

"Oh, do let's have some of those!" Alexandria sniffed the frigid air and then slipped and slid her way toward the stall from which the tantalizing smell of roasting oysters drifted out to entice the passers-by. She had already pulled her coin purse from her reticule when Harry caught up with her.

158

"Put that away," he growled, reaching underneath his greatcoat.

"Oh, no, I wish to pay." Her face was serious as she whispered up at him. "You cannot imagine the pleasure I derive from being able to. You see, I've never had any money to waste on fripperies before."

He shrugged and pulled his hand out empty, ignoring the look of contempt the fishmonger cast in his direction as Alexandria carefully counted out the correct change. After that he allowed her to treat him to brandy-balls and gingerbread, remarking that he was rapidly growing used to being "kept" and found it rather comfortable.

She laughed in reply and dragged him off to a skittle alley, where he beat her soundly. "Just to restore my sense of manhood," he explained, his face entirely serious except for the twinkle in his eyes.

While they were rummaging through the volumes of a book stall, she grabbed his arm. "Look there!" she hissed. "That man!"

"Where?" He turned and stared in the same direction. "What man?"

"Oh, he's gone into that crowd. Come on!" and she went dashing out of the book tent and down the mall with Harry hard bent to catch up with her.

"Whom are we chasing?" he panted. "Did someone snatch your purse while my back was turned?"

"No, of course not. I just thought I saw—though surely not—oh, it *is* he." And she came to a dead halt before one of the hastily erected gambling stalls where the Wheel of Fortune was spinning enticingly as the crowds collected to lay their wagers on its fate. "See over there, standing by the wheel. It's Mr. Roker."

It was indeed. The gambler who had enlivened their wedding night in the inn near Gretna Green was just shoving his winnings into his pockets. He either felt their stare or heard Alexandria say his name, for he raised his head and glanced their way. They had the uncomfortable experience of seeing his features startled into looking murderous before he brought his expression back to its usual gambler's blandness.

Roker elbowed his way through an eager crowd clamoring to share his luck while the wheel seemed so benevolent. He tipped his tall hat to them. "Well, well, as folk are always remarking, it's a queer, small world." He then smiled his formula smile, all teeth and gums and lips, leaving the rest of his facial anatomy uncommitted.

"I see you've been having marvelous luck," Alexandria remarked nervously, wondering what on earth had possessed her to pursue this villain. Curiosity, she supposed, and reminded herself of the bleak fate of the cat.

"It happens," Mr. Roker remarked jovially. "Dame Fortune's a fickle mistress, for a fact, but she does have a way sometimes of evening up the score. Now, when I last saw you folk, my luck couldn't've been rottener. But this time I couldn't seem to do much wrong."

"I noticed that," Harry remarked. "A suspicious sort of fellow might even suspect that your luck defied belief. You weren't trying to persuade all these people to risk their blunt, by any chance? Work here, do you?"

"Well, now." Mr. Roker lost all pretense at amiability and sneered down at Harry from his two-inch height advantage. "I'm not surprised to find you numbered among the suspicious types you referred to. Anybody who is up to as many tricks to rob an honest gambler of his stake as you and your missus here is bound to be suspicious. But just to set the record straight, no. I don't work here. Leastways, not in the way you mean it. I own the place."

"You've come up in the world, then. So my wife and I didn't do you that much disservice, after all. I'm glad to hear it."

"No, indeed." Roker smiled his chilling smile again. "Fact of the matter is, I'd say you did me a favor in the long run. For, Roker, I told myself, if you can let yourself be fleeced by a couple of gentry-coves still wet behind the ears, you really are a green-un. So I decided to come to London to educate myself. And I don't mind saying you couldn't work your little game on me a second time."

"But we didn't plan—" Alexandria began in protest, but Harry cut her short.

"You aren't going to convince Mr. Roker that you didn't gull him intentionally, so don't even try," he said. "Besides, we've interfered with his work too long already. Your servant, sir." He tipped his beaver politely to the gambler and led Alexandria away.

"That man really dislikes us." She shivered when they were out of sight.

"Oh, did you want him for a friend?" he asked, obviously wishing to forget the unpleasant Mr. Roker. "I say, are you game to try the swings?"

"If you are." She laughed joyously, also wiping the odious gambler from her mind while she and Harry threaded their way through the crowd, hand in hand, toward a wooden structure they could

161

barely see for the people thronged about it waiting their turns.

"Do you suppose it's safe?" Alexandria whispered as they edged up close. Two tall wooden A's were connected by a cross bar from which was suspended a curved boat-like swing that held four people while two burly men pushed them from either end. The entire contraption was mounted on a wooden platform.

"Of course it's safe," Harry answered, just as one of the occupants let out a piercing shriek.

After several couples had come reeling off the ride, clinging to one another and laughing hysterically, it was the Romneys' turn. While the swingers held the cradle steady, they climbed aboard and took the seat opposite a very skinny woman and a man who was all chins and belly. "At least they balance," Harry remarked underneath his breath. Alexandria laughed, staring intently as she did so at the waiting crowd so as not to give offense to their fellow passengers.

"Hold tight!" the operators yelled and gave a lusty push as Alexandria responded with a shriek that set Harry chuckling in her ear. It was most exhilarating, swinging high above the heads of the people at the Frost Fair, with the sharp wind nipping cheeks and nose and the colorful pageantry that flanked the river spreading out before their eyes. But it was also a bit scary, this dizzying back and forth above the heads of earth-bound folk, and Alexandria lacked perfect faith that the entire platform would not suddenly go sliding across the river like an ice boat or, worse yet, that an extra-lusty push would not send the swing circling above the bar and spill them like apples from an upturned box. She clutched at Harry as she squealed and he threw an arm protectively around her and held her close.

It was odd, then, how quickly she became lost to all sense of danger, and how the icy wind subsided to a glow of warmth. She looked up at Harry once and smiled and felt a current pass between them that she quickly attributed to the exhilaration of the ride. It was harder, though, to account for the expression on his face, which had lost its usual harshness. His dark eyes held hers in a look that she later tried to fathom and could not. Still, it seemed a magic moment. But then the pendulum they swung in gradually decreased its arc until the two controlling men stopped it altogether.

"That was fun," Alexandria remarked with some constraint as Harry helped her from the swing. She was already beginning to doubt the validity of her senses, to feel that she'd only imagined the electricity between them. Or, worse yet, that it had not been a feeling shared, but some odd response to Harry's nearness that she'd experienced all alone. That was, indeed, a lowering thought. She glanced at him uneasily and could not find even a trace of the imagined tenderness in his eyes. In fact, he was looking at her quite quizzically, as if trying to fathom what was going on in her mind. If anything, his eyes were cynical.

"Still dizzy?" he inquired.

"A little, I believe," she answered, subdued now that all the excitement seemed at an end. "I expect we should look for Evelyn. It's time I went home."

"I'll take you," he answered. "We'd never find them in this crowd, even if they're still here. Which I greatly doubt."

"You don't think—" She looked up, alarmed.

"No, I do not," he answered firmly, and then he grinned. "But I do think Evelyn will make a wonderful story of it when he goes back home. I can imagine the locals in the taverns all agog to hear how he toured the fair in the company of London's most lovely Cyprian. Evelyn won't lose his virtue, but his friends will never know it."

He found a carriage to take them home. But even though its drafty interior did not really provide much shelter from the cold, they did not draw close together and renew the intimacy of the swing, but rather sat self-consciously apart while they commented in a stilted manner on this or that experience at the fair.

"I'd like about a gallon of hot chocolate, wouldn't you?" Alexandria asked as the coachman pulled to a halt in Grosvenor Square.

"I'd prefer hot rum, but I'll settle for the other," he answered, helping her out, paying off the driver, and running with her up the steps.

As they breathlessly reached the welcoming warmth of the entrance hall, she turned to him impulsively. "I don't know when I've ever had quite so much fun. Certainly not since I've been in London. And, needless to say, at Lady Augusta's—"

"You mean I have actually been more entertaining than Aunt Augusta?" His eyes laughed at hers as he clapped a hand dramatically above his heart. "Woman, you may undo me with your lavish praise."

"Goose!" She laughed. "Oh, Padgett, could we please have chocolate?" she said as the butler suddenly materialized. "Boiling would be acceptable."

"Certainly, madam. In fact, cook is just preparing

a tea tray for Sir Oliver. He has been waiting for some time in the parlor."

Harry, who had been shrugging out of his greatcoat, swore underneath his breath. "My cousin seems more at home here than I do," he remarked in an offhand manner to Alexandria.

"Indeed, he rarely comes." But she had unaccountably been made uncomfortable. "I cannot imagine why he is here now."

"Can you not?" Harry answered, now buttoning his greatcoat up again.

"But aren't you going to have your chocolate? You must be frozen!"

"As I was saying, I'd actually prefer brandy punch. Or hot rum. The urge is suddenly overpowering."

"I'm sure that cook could manage."

"Cook could never hope to equal Watier's. So, if you'll excuse me? And, of course, give my best to Cousin Oliver." He bowed sardonically and left.

Alexandria stood still for a moment staring at the closed front door. Then she slowly turned away and climbed the stairs.

Chapter Fifteen

THE HONORABLE EVELYN COMBE WAS TRYING HARD to convey the impression that he was finding his first visit to Almack's decidedly on the flat side. After all, since he had initially gone into transports over the prospect of the Assemblies, had he not been to White's, Watier's, a masque-ball in Covent Garden, a rat pit, a cock-fight, a horse race, and a mill? And had he not spent an entire afternoon in the company of a fashionable impure?

Alexandria glanced at him with some amusement as they stood together at the conclusion of a dance and quizzed the other occupants of the ballroom. Evelyn was having some difficulty maintaining his studied boredom, a pose she'd have bet a monkey that he aped from Harry. Excitement would creep into his voice and betray him as he spied one notable after another in the room. "Look!

There's old 'Silence' Jersey herself, is it not? Lord, could she really ever have had Prinny dancing attendance upon her? It's beyond belief. Still, he's hardly an Adonis himself, come to think of it. But he is the Regent!"

"I understand that Lady Jersey was quite a handsome woman."

"Perhaps," the seventeen-year-old returned doubtfully, "but she's certainly past it now. Oh, look, there's the Duke of Sussex!" To Alexandria's relief, Evelyn finally abandoned his Byronic jadedness altogether. "I say, that's Miss Calcraft, is it not, who just came in there?" He teetered back and forth on tiptoe trying to see over the heads in the ballroom crush until he was satisfied that it was, indeed, the young beauty he'd met a few days before and had talked of incessantly ever since. His eyes sparkled with animation, making him appear just what he was, a nice, reasonably attractive youth having a marvelous holiday in London. "I say, you won't mind if I desert you, will you, Alex?" The question was merely asked for form's sake and she smiled the answer. "Good. I'm off to ask her to partner me. Wish me luck."

Alexandria was about to seek a seat when her hand was claimed. After that she never seemed to lack for partners, a circumstance she laid entirely at the feet of the hired hairdresser who had curled her hair so becomingly and to the credit of her pale blue crepe ball gown with its modish French bead edges.

But she had certainly not expected to find Oliver among the beaux asking to stand up with her. He was looking even more devastatingly handsome than usual in his frilled shirt, black long-tailed coat, and white knee britches. "I did not think to see you here," she blurted.

"But I trust you are not sorry," he said softly, giving her the slow, sad smile that for some reason failed to move her quite as much as formerly.

"No, of course not. It's just that with Amelia so—uh—delicate, I had not expected—"

"Amelia is not with me," he answered stiffly as they took their places in the set. "I have come for the purpose of escorting her sister Arabel."

"Arabel is in London?" The question was certainly fatuous, but she preferred it to her urge to giggle. "Shopping the marriage mart, is she, then?"

"I would not have expressed it in quite that way," he answered. "Her main concern is to be with her sister now that Amelia is going to have a child. They are very close, you know. But, then, one need not be blind to the advantages of London over the country with its limited society when it comes to making an eligible alliance."

"Yes." Alexandria looked round the Assembly Room with interest. "There must be any number of gazetted fortune hunters here." She laughed.

"Really, Alexandria," Oliver said reprovingly. "Such levity at the expense of others does not become you. I can see that my cousin Harry is a deplorable influence."

"I think not," she answered. "At least I don't see how he can have much influence upon me, deplorable or otherwise, for I rarely see him. You must know that. It's the *on-dit* of London."

"Even so," he continued in the same repressive tone, "I do not think you formerly would have made sport of Lady Arabel."

"Perhaps not. Governesses and hired companions

are not noted for their frivolity. But I did not intend to slight Lady Arabel by implying she may be the target of fortune hunters. Indeed, I find her position enviable. But let us change the subject. Pray tell me about Lord Woolridge's political success. While I heard that his bill passed, I know none of the particulars."

Their position in the set gave Oliver ample time to launch into a low but animated account of how various members of Parliament had been talked around to cast their votes in favor of the bill. Oliver modestly mentioned his own contribution here, mostly within the sphere of his wife's family influence, Alexandria noted, and spoke of the success of Lord Woolridge's speech, several passages of which, he mentioned, had been penned by his lordship's new secretary.

Their heads were close together to allow them to converse underneath the music. And, even though her attention was rather prone to wander, she tried hard to keep a rapt expression on her face. And so, she afterwards supposed, they must have conveyed an impression of cozy intimacy while Harry Romney watched them from across the room.

How long he had been there, she had no idea. Knowing his views on the deadliness of an evening spent at Almack's, she was amazed to see him among the company. She flashed him a smile of welcome, but since he was in the process of turning away, he evidently did not see her, though for some reason Alexandria got the distinct impression that he had.

When the set was finished and Oliver had thanked her formally and gone in search of Lady Arabel, Alexandria sat fanning herself for a moment from the heat of her exertions, expecting Harry to come to her. When it became obvious that he had no such intent, she made her way in his direction. He was just completing a conversation with an elderly acquaintance. He turned away and almost collided with Alexandria.

"I thought if I placed myself in a position to be stepped on, you might notice and stand up with me."

"I noticed you, all right," he replied without much warmth.

"Or, better still, take me to the refreshment saloon. I'm ready to die of thirst."

"Indeed? I'm amazed that your gallant escort would allow you to get into such dire straits."

"My gallant escort, as you term him, could not care a fig. He's too busy pursuing young ladies straight from the schoolroom to worry about an ancient like myself."

"Schoolroom misses? Oliver? I am astonished!"

"Certainly not Oliver. Evelyn, of course. How could you think I would have come to Almack's with Oliver?" she asked indignantly.

"It's a natural enough assumption. He seems constantly in your pocket. Every time I go to Grosvenor Square I find him camped there. And you must admit you were having a cozy *tête-à-tête* just now. I'm surprised you were actually able to tear yourselves away from your fascinating conversation long enough to participate in the dance."

"Really, you and Oliver are the outside of enough! One would think that you both would have outgrown your childish jealousies. And to put me in the middle of them is absurd. Most of that *tête-à-tête*, as you term it, consisted of his reading me a

170

lecture about allowing you to corrupt me into a display of levity. Which is as absurd as your saying he is constantly in my pocket. The truth is, I rarely see either of you. Oliver had actually come to see *you* on the day of the Frost Fair, as you would have discovered if you had stayed."

"And you believed that Banbury Tale? He knows I'm rarely there."

"He had family business to discuss and, since he happened to be passing by, he took a chance. But I really see no need to defend his conduct. We are cousins and he certainly may call upon me without impropriety. Now could we get some lemonade?" Suddenly she looked stricken. "Oh," she said in a small voice. "Did you come here to see someone in particular? I had forgotten the terms of our agreement. Am I intruding in your life? I am being very thoughtless."

In answer, he took her arm and steered her almost roughly toward the refreshment room. As he did so, he looked her up and down. "That gown needs jewels to set it off," he said abruptly. "Remind me to go through my mother's things and select something for you."

"Thank you very much. I had not known I looked so unbecoming."

"Don't fish. You're well aware that you look stunning. But you surely can't have missed the fact that you are practically the only woman here who is not wearing at least a string of pearls."

"In fact, I'm a reproach to the Romneys, you might say."

"Not likely." He gave her a quelling look. "What I might say is, it's a shame for my mother's jewelry not to be worn. I'll see to it. My God!" He had handed her a cup of lemonade and now took a sip of his. "I didn't think this pap could possibly be as bad as I remembered it. It's worse."

She laughed. "You certainly are not the stuff of martyrs. What did bring you here, by the way?"

She was never to hear the answer, for his attention was focused across the room and he was frowning in displeasure. "You have a strange notion of young ladies straight from the schoolroom, Alex. Evelyn would have to look long and hard to find a more knowing one than that."

She followed his gaze and sighted Evelyn listening with a rapt expression to a very sophisticated-looking woman of little more than her own age wearing a satin gown that not only left most of her milky bosom bare but also clung revealingly to her voluptuous figure. The woman was obviously flirting with Evelyn outrageously while he blushed in delighted embarrassment.

"Goodness, who is that?" Alexandria asked. "He left me in hot pursuit of a Miss Calcraft, who is a schoolroom miss, I assure you. Evelyn spied her in the park the other day and has talked of little else since."

"That is Maria Calcraft. Lady Calcraft." Harry's tone of voice caused Alexandria to look up at him wonderingly. "I expect that the girl you refer to is her sister-in-law. This is just the sort of thing Maria Calcraft might enjoy—stealing a halfling away from a young, inexperienced chit. Evelyn's obviously riding for a fall."

"He does look smitten, doesn't he?"

"Like a damned moon-calf."

"You—er—I take it—know the lady very well?"

Alexandria was obviously fishing and was not surprised to receive a quelling look.

"Better than I'd wish to. Let's just say that we were at one time rather close—for my sins. I'd as soon see Evelyn in the company of a viper."

"Goodness, you do dislike her!" Alexandria exclaimed. "And I'd give a monkey to know why," she finished candidly. "But you aren't going to tell me, are you?"

"No, I am not. Except to say that I am not in the habit of holding scheming, heartless females in high esteem. For instance, the gossip-mongers have it that her husband is having financial difficulties. In fact, that the poor devil is completely all to pieces. But she hardly looks grief-stricken for him, does she?"

"My heavens, if her character is as black as all of that, should you not warn Evelyn?"

"Do you think he'd listen?"

"Possibly not, but at least you'd have the satisfaction of knowing you had tried. Perhaps we should join them."

Harry gave her a look that made it quite plain he considered that a shatter-brained idea. He was prevented from elaborating, however, by the fact that Lady Arabel Fielding and Sir Oliver Linnell were approaching them with lemonade in hand.

Lady Arabel, Alexandria noted, was dressed in a many-flounced and very tamboured vivid yellow that increased rather than diminished her proportions. Nor did her ornate emerald necklace do much to tone her down. It did effectively advertise her wealth, though, Alexandria thought, and was immediately ashamed of herself.

Oliver greeted them with the usual constraint

173

Harry's presence always placed upon him. "You, of course, are already acquainted with my wife's sister," he said formally.

Lady Arabel gave the clear impression that only generations of good breeding made it possible for her to speak civilly, causing Alexandria to recall painfully the humiliation on both sides of their former meeting. "You cannot imagine my surprise," the younger Miss Fielding said haughtily, "when Oliver told me of your sudden marriage."

"It was, in fact, a surprise to everyone," Oliver remarked.

"Allow me to convey my felicitations."

If Harry doubted Lady Arabel's sincerity, Alexandria noticed, he quite failed to give himself away. In fact, he practically beamed down at her, a circumstance that discomposed the lady far more than his former indifference had.

"Thank you," he said with a smile. "I can understand your surprise, of course. Few people realize just how long I have felt a *tendre* for Alexandria. But the truth is, I have been enslaved by her since we were children. And I fear that my devotion quite prevented me from paying the proper attention due to others of the fair sex."

Alexandria choked suddenly and turned her head away. She studiously avoided looking up at Harry, for fear that she might indulge in a fit of the hysterics. She could not decide whether he'd made his preposterous statement just for the fun of being so outrageous in front of Oliver or from a genuine desire to smooth over his former slight to Lady Arabel. She hoped it might be the latter. For Alexandria suspected that Lady Arabel, despite her haughty ways, was capable of being hurt.

174

If Harry was indeed trying to be diplomatic, it most certainly was working. Lady Arabel thawed perceptibly. "I must admit that I am astonished to find you so romantic." She gave Harry a shy smile that made her look quite nice, or so Alexandria thought.

"Not nearly so astonished as I am," Oliver chimed in. "Now, if you will excuse us? Arabel is promised to Lord Elliston for the next set." He bowed stiffly and they took their leave.

"Of all the falsehoods I ever heard! A *tendre* for me since childhood! Really, Harry, that was outrageous!"

"It's true," he answered, his dark eyes mocking. "Ever since I drew Oliver's cork that day and you began to beat me with your stick, I've been yours."

"Fustian," she began, but was prevented from enlarging upon the theme by the appearance of her next partner, who had come to claim her hand for the boulanger that was just forming.

As the dance concluded, she finally got the opportunity to look around for Harry, but she found that he had gone. At that point she mentally pronounced the Assembly at Almack's to be every bit as flat as Evelyn had pretended it to be.

Chapter
Sixteen

W HEN PADGETT INFORMED ALEXANDRIA A FEW
days later that a parcel had arrived for her
from the jeweler, she thought there was some mistake.

"I have not ordered anything," she said, taking
the flat, rectangular package from his hand.

"There's a card with it, madam."

She waited until he had rather reluctantly left
the parlor to read the message. "I've had my mother's diamonds reset for you. I hope they're in your
style. Harry." She smiled first at the bold, hasty
scrawl, then eagerly tore off the string and opened
up the parcel.

"Ooooh!" She sat down suddenly, staring in disbelief as the loveliest necklace she had ever seen
soaked up the feeble rays of morning light, magni-
fied them, and dazzled her eyes like sun on snow.

"Ooooh," she whispered again. "How exquisite!" Then she snatched up box and necklace and paper and string and went racing into her bedchamber, where she quickly slid out of her high-yoked muslin gown with its gathered trimming underneath the chin and stood before the cheval glass in her petticoat, clasping the necklace round her throat. "Ooooh," she breathed yet again, her eyes sparkling like the diamonds.

For the rest of the day Alexandria walked in a daze, making frequent trips to her dressing-table drawer just to be sure she had not dreamed it all. She tried in vain to chide herself for her vanity. She would not have thought that the necklace could affect her so. And, indeed, it was not the monetary worth of the jewels that overwhelmed her, though she realized its value must be staggering. It was simply the fact that this necklace was a work of art, of exquisite craftsmanship, the simplicity of the setting yielding precedence to the perfectly cut stones, allowing them the maximum of beauty freed from all distractions. Nor could she forget that the diamonds themselves were heirlooms, handed down for generations in Harry's mother's family. And now they had come to her.

Evelyn, stopping by Grosvenor Square between engagements, was suitably impressed. He gave a long, low whistle. "Oh, I say! I knew Harry was a nabob, but this defies belief."

"He didn't buy it. It's been in his family for donkeys' years. He did have it reset though. Do you think that was terribly expensive?" she asked anxiously.

"Not as compared to paying for all these sparklers," Evelyn said, tallying up the diamonds, then not quite believing his arithmetic and counting them again.

"Well, now, isn't this a stroke of luck," he added. "You can wear the necklace to Drury Lane. Of course, if you do, no one will look at that Kean fellow, but that's his hard luck."

"Oh? I did not know I was going to Drury Lane."

"Of course you didn't, you goose. I stopped by to tell you. But then you brought out your treasure chest and put me off. Lady Calcraft has asked us to join her in her box."

"Lady Calcraft? Oh, is Miss Jane Calcraft to be among the number then?" Alexandria could have bitten her tongue as Evelyn turned red.

"No. At least I do not think so. She and her sister-in-law are not exactly bosom-beaux. They have little in common, actually, so Maria says." Alexandria took note of his first-name usage as Evelyn went on to explain that Miss Calcraft was rather sweet but hopelessly green, a girl whom a sophisticate like Maria was bound to find a deadly bore. "But Maria most particularly wishes to become known to you and insisted that I bring you." If the Queen had requested her company for tea, Alexandria thought, Evelyn would not have been nearly so impressed.

Her resolve to observe at close range just what sort of game the worldly Lady Calcraft was playing made Alexandria decide to accept the theater invitation. She felt it her family duty to rescue her husband's stepbrother from the clutches of a practiced siren if it proved necessary. Besides, Evelyn was right, of course. Here was a perfect opportunity to dazzle polite society with her gorgeous necklace.

And, indeed, after she and Evelyn had been ushered into Lady Calcraft's theater box that evening and introductions had been made, it did become the immediate topic of conversation. "What a lovely necklace you are wearing!" the hostess exclaimed while her shrewd dark eyes appraised it.

"Thank you. It belonged to my husband's mother. He has just had the stones reset, however."

Lady Calcraft's finely arched eyebrows rose. "La, I am surprised," she drawled. "Both at Harry being so industrious and at the former Lady Woolridge possessing anything so valuable. I know that uncle of hers was wealthy, of course, but the rest of the family never seemed to have a feather to fly with."

Alexandria gave her hostess a frosty smile. She was taking an intense dislike to Lady Maria Calcraft, whether over her veiled slur of Harry's family or because of her familiar use of his name, Alexandria could not decide.

"And where is our dear Harry tonight?" the beauty went on to inquire with a small, knowing smile. "Since his ladybird has flown, I can't imagine why he would leave the side of his pretty young bride so soon after the wedding ceremony."

Alexandria seethed at the woman's audacity in openly referring to Harry's mistress. "My husband and I prefer to maintain a certain independence," she replied pleasantly, though her hands were clenched tightly beneath her fan. "I wished to spend some time with Evelyn, and Harry, I'm afraid, doesn't always ... appreciate ... the company his stepbrother keeps. In fact, tonight when he heard we would be attending the theater with you, he suddenly recalled a previous engagement. Perhaps you can explain his behavior better than I,

Lady Calcraft." She let her voice trail off suggestively.

Alexandria was pleased to see the beauty's pale skin flush an angry red. But, with a tight smile, Lady Calcraft replied, "Indeed, I cannot. But you are so young, my dear, such an innocent about all matters of life. And Harry is so *very* experienced, so *very* skilled . . . Is it any wonder he becomes easily bored?" She paused significantly. "Did he ever mention, by chance, that he and I were quite . . . close . . . at one time?"

Lady Calcraft's blatant allusion to her affair with Harry, as well as her implication that Alexandria was too inexperienced to interest him as a lover, made her, for some reason, want to push the woman over the balcony and into the pit far below. Without considering the source of her rage, she determined not to disgrace Harry by losing her temper.

Evelyn interrupted at that moment with a silly comment intended as a witticism, thereby allowing Alexandria to refrain from replying to Lady Calcraft's last remark. She gritted her teeth and stiffened her resolve to extract Evelyn from the siren's clutches just as quickly as she could.

This would be no easy task, however, she concluded, as she had more opportunity to observe Evelyn in the beauty's presence. That he was in the grip of his first calf-love was evident. It was also evident that Lady Calcraft was doing everything within her power to encourage his infatuation. To what purpose, Alexandria could not imagine.

There might have been some initial satisfaction in spiriting Evelyn away from her pretty young sister-in-law. But once that had been accomplished,

Alexandria could not imagine why Lady Calcraft continued to encourage him to dangle after her. Evelyn was neither strikingly handsome nor very rich, and was a second son at that. And certainly Lady Calcraft did not look for beaux, Alexandria had observed as she was introduced to the other members of the party. Besides the hostess and herself, there was only one other female present: a Mrs. Brice, whose husband was on the continent and whose reputation was barely short of scandalous. The rest of the party was made up of males of all ages from young to ancient, every last one of whom seemed smitten by Lady Calcraft. Indeed, it was a lesson in coquetry, Alexandria noted with a contempt that was not quite free of envy, to observe how skillfully the lady played each against the others.

Even so, Alexandria soon began to suspect that some other common interest besides devotion to Lady Calcraft had brought this group together. This became quite evident when only she among the occupants of the box fell victim to the magic spell being woven for them upon the stage.

Drury Lane Theater was packed from its gallery to its pit. The play-going public had turned out in droves to see the new controversial thespian who had all London agog, an actor recently arrived from playing in the provinces, the unique and up-and-coming Edmund Kean.

Lady Calcraft had chosen Thursday night for her theater party since Kean would be playing *Richard III*, the part that most critics felt showed him at his best. At first, Alexandria felt decidedly let down as the curtain rose to disclose a small, dark, unprepossessing figure bustling across the stage. She

181

had finally had the opportunity to see Kemble act at Covent Garden and a greater contrast to his tall, commanding presence and heroic style could not be imagined. And she was certainly not the first to think so. Indeed, Kean's reading of Richard's line, "But that I am not shaped for sportive tricks," was delivered with such an ironical twist that he, too, must have had the inevitable comparison with England's premier actor in his mind.

A whisper had swept the theater as Kean proceeded to speak Shakespeare's opening soliloquy in natural tones rather than to declaim it, but the murmurings soon hushed as the audience succumbed to the spell of this strange original of whom Coleridge had written, "To see him act, is like reading Shakespeare by flashes of lightning."

At the first-act curtain it became apparent to Alexandria that despite the interest shown by the rest of the audience, their party was merely filling time waiting for the main attraction of the evening, whatever that might be. And when the fourth-act curtain dropped, the octogenarian of the group suggested that they leave right then and avoid the later crush. Alexandria's, "Oh, dear, must we?" was lost in the general clamor of approval from all the other occupants of the box.

Her disappointment in being wrenched away from the electrifying performance upon the stage soon turned to deep disgust when she discovered, if she rightly understood, that they were rushing from the theater in order to play at cards at Lady Calcraft's. Alexandria could not imagine anything more tedious and gave a hopeful look around the other boxes before they left, trying to discover someone she knew well enough to join. But she looked in vain for the Linnells or for Lord Woolridge. And she'd known from the very first that Harry was not among the throng packed into Drury Lane.

She toyed with the idea of asking Evelyn to take her home, then quickly gave it up. He would certainly resent being parted from Maria Calcraft for the time it took. Besides, Alexandria felt dutybound not to forsake her self-appointed post as chaperone to her young friend.

Even when she saw the butler at the Calcraft residence in Hanover Square, Alexandria only considered it another evidence of her hostess's eccentricity that she should employ someone who looked like a pugilist instead of the usual refined-looking type of upper servant. The theater group had deposited their cloaks with this strange personage and proceeded upstairs to the first story before Alexandria became aware that Lady Calcraft was also playing hostess to other guests. Indeed, from the din of voices and the clink of glasses she thought all of society not left at Drury Lane must be gathered there.

But it was not until they entered the first saloon and the dozen or so persons seated round a card table did not so much as glance their way, that it dawned upon Alexandria that the Calcraft residence was nothing more than a genteel gaminghouse.

She had heard of such places. In fact, there had been some recent articles in the newspapers about the wickedness of trying to cloak gambling under the guise of respectability. A gaming-hell is a gaming-hell, had been one article's conclusion, whether located in a gentleman's parlor in St. James's Square or openly situated in Pall Mall.

These upper-class establishments were usually run by persons of the ton who were themselves addicted to games of chance, or by those attempting to recoup their own lost fortunes. And the two conditions most often went together.

Alexandria recalled Harry's remark about Sir Peter Calcraft being all to pieces. But surely if Harry had heard of Lady Calcraft's antidote for her husband's bankruptcy, he would have mentioned it. She wondered if Evelyn had known what they were letting themselves in for. From the guilty look he sent her way, she rather thought he had.

Alexandria evidently had not hidden her dismay. "You're looking quite amazed." Her hostess seemed to be enjoying a private joke. "Don't tell me this is your first visit to a polite gaming-house. I'm surprised that Harry has kept you quite so sheltered. It's very shabby of him, considering his own predilection for faro and deep basset. But then you and Harry have the perfect marriage, have you not? You rarely see one another."

Alexandria was determined not to let the woman get the best of her. "The fact that Harry and I are rarely together," she began with perfect equanimity, "makes the times when we *are* together all that much more enjoyable, Lady Calcraft. A woman of your ... uh ... varied background will appreciate, I'm sure, that anticipation is half the fun. But perhaps, in your case, you've been kept waiting too long."

"Not at all, Mrs. Romney," Alexandria's nemesis replied coldly, the light of battle snapping in her eyes. "I've simply gone on to pleasures more to my liking." Her gloved hand indicated the gaming tables in a grand gesture. "Now, won't you join your brother-in-law?" she asked, her eyes on Evelyn in the next room, where a faro bank was operating.

"No, thank you. I fear I'm no hand at cards."

"Well, then, roulet should be more to your liking. We've only recently acquired a table. We're rather proud of it and like to show it off." She cut short any protest that Alexandria might be forming. "It will help you pass the time. I expect Evelyn will be occupied for quite a while. And, though we pride ourselves that our suppers are the best in London, it will be at least one hour before we serve."

Alexandria trailed reluctantly after Lady Calcraft. They entered the same saloon Evelyn had vanished into, and, in spite of her disgust, Alexandria was struck by its elegance. The walls were lined in a cool green silk and adorned with heavy brocade window hangings. Rosewood card tables in the Egyptian taste with bronzed legs and gilt enrichments were placed strategically throughout the room. These were accompanied by a profusion of gilt armchairs designed with comfortable caned seats and backs.

The gamesters at one of the card tables were making room for Evelyn, and the rest of the theater party was being assimilated into other play. In contrast to the deathly seriousness of the card game in the first saloon, a party mood prevailed in one corner of this room. There was much whooping and laughter and good-natured groaning as the players watched with rapt attention the gyrations of a little ball within a spinning wheel. Lady Calcraft ushered Alexandria into this group.

"Sir Hubert will explain the game," she drawled,

smiling in a conspiratorial manner at the ancient who had been with them in the box at Drury Lane. She then excused herself and went to speak to her other guests.

At least this particular pastime did not seem to require much skill, Alexandria noted thankfully. All that the participants appeared to do was to hazard their money and watch the wheel. And, of course, follow the results with appropriate squeals or groans. She did hope it was not going to prove quite expensive. Not that she need worry too much, of course. She had spent very little of the pin money Harry had allowed her. Well, she certainly had no desire to waste it now in this silly way, but there seemed to be no help for it.

"Would you care to place your bet, Mrs. Romney?"

Alexandria started at the familiar voice. She had been so absorbed in watching the movements of the little ball and the reactions of the players that she had not really looked at the large man in evening clothes who was setting the wheel in motion.

"Do you wish to play, Mrs. Romney?" Mr. Roker said again, giving her his wolfish smile.

"I-I suppose so," she answered weakly. "Of course, I've never done so before."

"Are you sure?" Mr. Roker laughed knowingly. "But then, of course, you would not gull me; it's just that I once made the mistake of believing your husband had never played piquet."

The octogenarian took it upon himself to be her mentor, and the game certainly did seem simple enough. Alexandria punted, the ball went into the proper slot, and she was congratulated loudly on her luck.

"You plan to take your winnings now and leave, do you not?" Mr. Roker remarked, a bit more loudly than seemed necessary. "You see, I have not forgot the Romney style of play."

"Of course she ain't thinking of anything so shabby," Alexandria's tutor said reprovingly.

"Well, now, that's just my and Mrs. Romney's little joke," the gambler said. "You'll let it ride, then?" Alexandria nodded.

After that Alexandria was so involved with keeping an eye upon Evelyn, who was never too absorbed in his own game not to watch the comings and goings of their hostess with a moon-struck expression on his face, that she failed to pay very much attention to the turning of the wheel. Besides, the octogenarian had taken over the management of her affairs, to both their satisfaction. From his pleased cackling and the frequent slaps he gave her shoulder, she gathered she was winning still. So it was quite a shock when Mr. Roker said, "You owe the bank five hundred pounds now, Mrs. Romney."

"I beg your pardon?"

"I'm afraid you heard me right, ma'am." Mr. Roker's tone was most regretful, but he did not bother to hide the pleasure of revenge glinting in his eyes.

"Been better if you'd stopped half an hour ago," the octogenarian remarked cheerfully. "We were winning then."

With some odd notion of not disgracing Harry running through her head, Alexandria tried her best not to show the panic she was feeling. "I haven't anywhere near that amount with me," she said to Mr. Roker. "You will accept my note?"

"Well, now, ma'am, we are not in the custom of doing that. Our ladies and gentlemen never punt beyond what they carry with them."

Alexandria opened her mouth to express her opinion of that preposterous statement, then quickly closed it once again.

"I tell you what you can do, though," Mr. Roker went on smoothly. "You can leave that necklace as security. It should cover your debt adequately."

"I most certainly will not leave it!" Alexandria's hand flew protectively to her throat. "My husband just gave it to me. It's worth far more than five hundred pounds and you well know it."

"As to that, I couldn't say." Mr. Roker shrugged. "But since you can have it back again once you pay up, there's no need to get into such a taking." Their voices had been pitched low throughout the exchange, but even so they were attracting a great deal of attention from the other patrons of the establishment.

"It's Jarrell Linnell's daughter," Alexandria heard someone whisper. "Must be in the blood."

"Just let me speak to Lady Calcraft," she said coldly. "I'm sure we can work out some more satisfactory arrangement."

Maria Calcraft was apparently all solicitude; nevertheless, Alexandria suspected that she was enjoying her guest's plight fully as much as Mr. Roker, if not more so. In fact, Alexandria was beginning to conclude that she'd been deliberately lured into the game.

"I can't imagine what Harry will say," Lady Calcraft commiserated. "He's not accustomed to losing, is he? But I'm sure you can bring him round.

After all, any man who'd give his wife such a valuable necklace is obviously still on his honeymoon."

"I wished to speak to you about the necklace. Mr. Roker insists upon it as security. Will you not take my note instead?"

"I'm terribly, terribly sorry," Lady Calcraft said, "but you see the roulet is Mr. Roker's own enterprise. I have nothing at all to say to that. He owns the table and merely pays me a commission on his winnings. But don't distress yourself. You can redeem your necklace in the morning. Harry need never know. Now, if you'll excuse me, I must see to supper."

There seemed nothing left to do but to leave the necklace and go home to spend a sleepless night. Even Evelyn was shocked by Alexandria's losses. "I say, Alex, you should have stopped before you got in so deep, you know."

"Mr. Roker does not approve of quitting while one is ahead," she replied bitterly.

Evelyn tried to console her that all would soon be right and tight. She'd only have to economize for several months, since her allowance was all spent, but she should not concern herself about the necklace. "Maria would never allow anyone in her house who wasn't on the up and up, you know." Alexandria could only wish that she shared his confidence.

The lawyer who handled Harry's business found her waiting in his office when he arrived the next day, and she was standing on Lady Calcraft's doorstep with five hundred pounds tucked into her reticule long before the hour for morning calls. After she'd been left cooling her heels in the reception hall for some twenty minutes, the burly butler returned to say that Lady Calcraft had not the faintest idea where Mr. Roker lived, but if Mrs. Romney would call this evening, she could then transact her business.

It appeared there was nothing more that Alexandria could do but go back home and wait out the seemingly neverending day. Then, with Evelyn recruited as her escort, she once again demanded entrance to the gaming-house.

"It's rather odd. Mr. Roker has never been so late before." Lady Calcraft's voice and eyes were mocking.

Even Evelyn seemed suddenly disenchanted with her. "We've been waiting two hours now. If you ask me, the fellow's done a bunk with Alexandria's necklace. What do you know about him?"

"Why, nothing, actually," she drawled. "Ours is a rather casual arrangement. This is, after all, a private home and not a business establishment."

"In other words, it's only your friends who are fleeced here," Evelyn said angrily.

"My friends are not so green as that," Lady Calcraft sneered. "Now, if you'll excuse me. And, by the by, I shall have to ask you either to play or to leave. You are upsetting my other guests."

"We'll leave all right," Evelyn retorted, flushing darkly. "And go straight for the Bow Street Runners."

"To what end?"

"To set after your colleague, naturally."

"Oh, I think not." Lady Calcraft smiled sweetly. "Mrs. Romney played roulet and lost it."

"She lost nowhere near the value of that necklace and you know it."

"Do I?" Lady Calcraft smiled again. "I think you'll find that difficult to prove."

"Come on, Evelyn," Alexandria said in a choking voice. "We're wasting our time here."

"It took you rather a long time to realize the obvious. But just one moment, Mrs. Romney." Lady Calcraft stepped over to a side table and extracted a pair of scissors from a drawer. Then she deliberately snipped off a lock of her raven hair, wrapped it in the wisp of handkerchief she carried, and handed it to Alexandria. "Do give that to Harry with my love. Tell him it's a replacement for the one he sent back to me."

Her eyes flashed in triumph as she turned on her heel and left.

Chapter
Seventeen

"OH, I SAY, ALEX, YOU DO LOOK AWFUL."
Alexandria did not doubt the truth of
Evelyn's tactless statement. Two sleepless nights
had taken their toll. Indeed, Evelyn's boyish face
looked strained and drawn as well. He'd set out
early from Brook Street in search of the elusive Mr.
Roker and had just come up to Alexandria's bedchamber to report. It was obvious from his expression that the news was bad.

"I did find his direction," he said rather proudly.
"I greased the palm of that villain Maria has
guarding her front door. Why we were such flats as
not to see through her little set-up the moment we
clapped eyes on that one, I'll never know," he interposed. "Anyhow, I bribed him to tell me where
Roker lived. He has a room near Covent Garden,
but of course he wasn't there. His landlady said

he'd been called away suddenly—a death in the family, so she thought. Said she had no reason to think, though, he'd not be back."

"Obviously she's never heard of the necklace, then," Alexandria remarked bitterly.

"So I guess all we can do is wait. Unless," he added diffidently, "you think I should tell Harry?"

"No!" They had discussed all this before. Alexandria remained adamant that they not tell Harry about the necklace until all else had failed. "Maybe what the landlady says is true. Perhaps there was a death in Roker's family."

"Perhaps." But Evelyn's voice carried no more conviction than she felt. He got up from the foot of her bed, where she lay exhausted, propped up by pillows, trying to coax away a pounding headache. "I say, Alex," he said, as he prowled nervously about the room, "won't Harry wonder why you ain't wearing the necklace at Carlton House?"

"I've thought of that. I shall say the clasp is broken and I've sent it for repairs."

"That's jolly good!" Evelyn looked at Alexandria admiringly while she herself reflected how quickly she'd gone from being a gamester to a liar. Perhaps that unknown person at the Calcrafts' had been right; it was in the blood.

But she held to her conviction that it was kinder to Harry in the long run to deceive him. She had not given him Maria Calcraft's lock of hair, but had enjoyed burning it instead. And when she'd explained its significance to Evelyn, there'd been the satisfaction of seeing the last spark of his calf-love die. "Maria only used us, then, to get back at Harry," he'd muttered with an oath that she pretended not to hear.

"Well," he said now, "I guess it will be best to say nothing till we're positive Roker isn't coming back. But I wonder if you can carry the thing off, Alex. One look at you and he's bound to know something's up. Look, I hate to say it, but if we haven't got the necklace back by the time of the fête, I think you will have to tell him."

She feared he was right. It really did seem the outside of enough that she and Harry, who never went anywhere together, were now engaged to do so. They were to take an active part in the general celebration that had been going on for weeks. For just as the great frost had finally given way to glorious spring, so had the bloody war waged so long and furiously upon the continent finally reached an end. The Prussians were in Paris, the English victorious at Toulouse, Napoleon was exiled upon Elba, and fat old Louis XVIII was once more King of France.

The victory had been followed by state visits from foreign royalty. The Grand Duchess Catherine of Russia came to England first. She and the Prince Regent took an immediate, violent dislike to one another. Then, when the Czar Alexander arrived some weeks afterwards, he refused to stay in St. James Palace and joined his sister Catherine in Pulteney's Hotel. Even King Frederick of Prussia did not fall in completely with the Regent's arrangements for him. He did go to Clarence House, but demanded that the satinwood furniture installed especially for him be removed and a spartan camp bed be set up in its place.

After several weeks of royal visits, the Regent was reported to be looking fagged and "tired of the whole thing." Indeed, the entire country had grown weary of the ungracious foreign guests and were ready to welcome their own heroes home. Now, at last, the Duke of Wellington was back on English soil.

Alexandria had been ecstatic when an invitation had arrived asking Mr. and Mrs. Romney to a fête at Carlton House in honor of the Duke. She'd stayed in a fever of suspense, fearing Harry would not wish to go. After all, Carlton House was no novelty for Harry. And she did not expect him to realize or care just how much she longed to see it. But evidently even the independent Mr. Romney did not feel free to decline the royal invitation, for he had sent her word that they'd attend. And she had been in raptures of anticipation until the night she lost the necklace. Now it was with a sinking heart that she came down the stairs to face her waiting husband.

At first she suspected that Harry's eyes were piercing right through the light evening cloak she wore and seeing her bare throat. He looked that harsh and grim. But as they rode down Bond Street in silence, she decided he scarcely even knew she was with him. Whatever was troubling Harry had nothing to do with the diamonds or with her. But, instead of being lifted, her spirits now sank even lower. How could she tell him she'd lost a necklace worth a fortune when his mood was already so cast down?

As their carriage slowed down to a tedious crawl, Harry pulled out of his lethargy long enough to ask, "Do you still feel honored by your invitation?"

She managed a little laugh. Two thousand guests had been asked for nine o'clock and the streets were clogged.

Eat, drink, and be merry, Alexandria thought as they finally arrived. She sought to put her troubles out of her mind. For she knew that, even if there were no disaster looming over her, she would never experience such as this again. Even Harry seemed to make an effort to shake off his gloom as they approached the grand entrance to the palace.

Indeed, a mood change proved not as difficult as she had feared, for to step through the Regent's portals was to leave all reality behind. "You can say you almost visited Carlton House," Harry whispered with a chuckle as they were ushered with hordes of other guests into the garden.

A special polygonal building had been put up there, for, typical of the Regent's extravagance, a mere tent would not suffice. This was a solid structure built of brick and topped with a leaded roof, but it gave the impression to the guests who filed inside that they were not indoors at all but in some magic garden in fairyland. Looking glasses hung with muslin draperies and sparkling from the illumination of twelve chandeliers gave a festive effect of summer light and airiness. Huge banks of artificial flowers shaped like a temple were arranged upon the floor. Two bands were concealed behind the foliage while music emerged as if by magic through the leaf-and-petal wall.

Nor was this all. Alexandria and Harry strolled leisurely down a covered promenade, decorated with draperies and rose-colored cords, that led to a Corinthian temple. There they joined the admiring throng gawking at a marble bust of the Duke of Wellington. The sculpture was placed upon a column in front of a large mirror engraved with a star and the letter *W*.

"My God, they've canonized him," a voice behind them said, and they turned to see three officers staring at their leader's likeness in amused disbelief.

"Come on," Harry said abruptly, and dragged Alexandria away.

They ambled slowly down a second walk. This one was decorated with green calico, its walls lined with allegorical transparencies representing "Military Glory," "The Overthrow of Tyranny by the Allied Powers," "The Arts of England," and the like. By the time they had emerged from viewing these, Alexandria had almost forgotten her troubles.

From there Harry led her on to a refreshment room hung with white and rose and festooned with regimental colors upon printed silk. Sipping champagne, talking and laughing with Harry's many friends, Alexandria found the evening passing much too quickly.

She was jerked back to reality once, however, when Harry remarked casually, "Why did you not wear your diamonds?"

She had thought that crisis passed some time before when she had removed the concealing wrap she wore and the question had not been asked. Now it shocked her off balance more than it might have done earlier. She thought of saying, "Because they were not suited to this gown," but it would not do. The simplicity of the satin dress she wore low on her bosom, with her shoulders bare, gave such a statement the immediate lie. Instead, she stumbled through her rehearsed speech about the broken clasp. Harry did not comment, but she knew he'd not been taken in by her deception. She hastily gulped down her champagne, desperately trying to regain a festive mood.

Wishing to look anywhere except at Harry's face, Alexandria glanced around the crowded refreshment tent, commenting mindlessly upon whatever oddity met her eye. Finally, made more desperate by Harry's lack of response to her stilted chatter, she tried a more direct approach. "Who is that distinguished officer who keeps staring at us?" She recognized him as the one who had been so amused by the bust of Wellington. "He must know you."

"More likely you have picked up another admirer." Harry's tone was not encouraging, nor was his black look as he followed her gaze to where the officer in question had now turned away from them to talk to his companion.

"Do you know him?" Alexandria asked as Harry continued to stare.

"I know who he is," he answered shortly.

"Who?" She was so desirous to get his mind off the necklace that she ignored the apparent desire on his part to drop the subject.

"Colonel O'Hara," he said repressively. "Aide-decamp to Wellington."

Her eyes opened wide at the name old Lady Augusta had given as Harry's true father and she looked stricken. Harry did not miss her embarrassment. "I see you've been listening to gossipmongers," he said dryly. "Let's move on."

No amount of champagne was able to restore Alexandria's spirits as they threaded their way through the crowds. "Look, there's your father," she said, relieved at having finally found a way to break the silence. Then she could have bitten off her tongue.

"Lord Woolridge, I presume you mean," Harry said sarcastically.

"Come, let's go speak to them," she answered, heading in the direction of Woolridge's party, giving Harry no choice but to follow her.

Lord Woolridge looked surprisingly glad to see them. He was with a group of Tory friends and Alexandria supposed he was happy to present his heir in the guise of a settled married man.

Sir Oliver and Lady Linnell were in his party and Alexandria noted with more surprise than envy how well the latter looked. Amelia was one of those rare females who really did grow lovelier with impending motherhood. Oliver's wife greeted them almost warmly, then went on to explain that, while she seldom appeared in public anymore, this was an occasion she could not bring herself to miss.

A bit later, when the conversation had grown more general, Alexandria managed to draw Oliver aside. "I must see you as soon as possible," she whispered. "In fact, I'm desperate to do so."

Oliver looked understandably startled but did not waste time with questions. "I'll call on you the first thing in the morning," he whispered back. "There'll be no chance tonight."

Alexandria turned away then, dismayed to find Harry standing at her elbow. His face had looked so forbidding all night long that it was impossible now to tell whether he had overheard or not.

The group soon separated, Harry having excused them from Woolridge's invitation to join his party by inventing a prior commitment for Alexandria and himself. The two strolled in strained silence for a while. It was with a sense of relief that at two o'clock they made their way into the supper tent.

The relief, however, was short-lived. Alexandria was engaged in gawking at the portly Regent who, adorned in a field marshal's full dress uniform, was seated at the head table in conversation with the Duke of Wellington. Harry was too concerned with finding places in the crowded supper tent to take note of their fellow diners. After they had been seated, one of these cleared his throat and they glanced across the table. "May I present myself?" the military gentleman asked. "I'm Colonel John O'Hara."

"Mr. and Mrs. Henry Romney," Harry answered shortly.

"Actually, I knew that." The colonel smiled disarmingly.

Harry looked nothing at all like him, was Alexandria's panicked first reaction. He was by far too good looking.

And indeed he was. Colonel O'Hara's red hair, lightly sprinkled now with grey, his blue eyes, and his easy smile all proclaimed his Celtic background.

"I'm by way of being a distant cousin of your mother's," the colonel said to Harry. "I knew her very well."

"So I have heard."

Colonel O'Hara looked slightly taken aback by Harry's curt reply but he pressed on. "Her untimely death was tragic. She was the most beautiful woman I ever saw." The words were polite platitudes, but for a moment Alexandria imagined she saw real grief reflected in the soldier's eyes for the long-dead beauty. But it quickly passed. The colonel turned her way with easy gallantry. "But then the Romney men seem to have formed a tradition of wedding beauties," he said, smiling.

Alexandria rallied to cover Harry's sullen silence with a series of skillful questions that kept the colonel chatting about his adventures on the continent, salted with frequent anecdotes of the colorful Iron Duke. Even so, the supper seemed interminable. She hardly tasted any of the delicacies piled high upon her plate and was only dimly aware that she was partaking freely of the iced champagne.

Finally the repast ended. Colonel O'Hara bent gallantly over Alexandria's hand, bowed briefly and formally to her husband, and went striding off.

"Do you think you can navigate?" Harry asked politely.

"Oh, yes," she answered, noting with dismay that her voice tended to sound rather indistinct. She'd been a gamester and a liar, and now she was a wine-bibber, she thought despondently. To her horror, she felt the sting of tears that threatened to overflow.

"Come on. I think I'd best get you home," Harry said. She glanced up at him then, expecting to find loathing for her condition written on his face. Instead, for the first time that evening, he looked amused. "I don't think you are really cut out for the high life, Alex," he remarked.

Avoiding their acquaintances, he steered her carefully through the crowd, retrieved her wrap, and secured a carriage for them. Then, having squired her safely to Grosvenor Square, he still deemed it necessary to escort her all the way up to her room and turn her over to the ministrations of her maid.

"Am I really cast-away, Harry?" Alexandria

asked, as the maid made haste to unfasten her evening gown.

"No, not cast-away exactly. A trifle up in the world I'd say."

"It's very lowering to be in this condition," she replied, and the tears that had been threatening her all evening now overflowed and went running down her cheeks.

"Oh, come now, Alex," Harry said, dabbing ineffectually at the tears with a snowy handkerchief. Was it only her imagination, or did the gesture hold more than a hint of tenderness? As the maid undid the last fastening, the gown slipped from Alexandria's shoulders, landing in a billow of satin at her feet. "Brace up," Harry added, his voice grown suddenly husky. "It can't really be as bad as all of that."

"That's where you are wrong." She'd finally managed to stop blubbering long enough to get the words out. But with a burning look at her partially exposed bosom, he turned and strode quickly from the room.

Chapter Eighteen

ALTHOUGH IT SEEMED HER HEAD HAD BARELY touched her pillow, Alexandria rose early the next morning to spend the day anxiously awaiting Oliver. As the hour grew later and later, she toyed with the idea of sending a message to him but was stopped by the obvious impropriety of such an act. Instead, she recalled one by one and with disgust his past declarations of devotion to her. He surely might have realized she would never have appealed to him had not her cause been desperate.

She had not come to that point without misgivings. But all her alternatives had been eliminated. Roker was never coming back. There was no more that a stripling like Evelyn could do to help her. She had even thought of going to Lord Woolridge with the story, but a horrified Evelyn had quickly put a damper on that notion. The respectable little lawyer who managed Harry's finances seemed equally unapproachable. Alexandria doubted that he'd ever come into contact with a sharper like Mr. Roker. And she would not, could not, turn to Harry yet. If all else failed, he would have to know eventually that she had lost an heirloom worth a fortune. But she would postpone that black day as long as possible. So she had made her desperate appeal to Oliver.

"What kept you?" she snapped when, in the late afternoon, he finally appeared. She'd been sitting in the library, the most private location for their interview. She had dropped the book she'd been holding just for form's sake and had jumped impatiently to her feet, her nerves raw with all the waiting. Nor did she now invite Oliver to sit down.

He looked understandably aggrieved at her reception. "I came as soon as I could," he said reproachfully. "You seem to have forgot that I was up all night at Carlton House. Also Amelia was unwell after all the excitement and I—"

"I'm sorry," Alexandria broke into his explanation. "It's just that I was so desperate to see you." To her horror, she broke into tears again.

"Oh, my dearest." Oliver moved closer and took her hand. His eyes, too, were moist and tender. "You mustn't break down this way. We must learn to disguise our feelings."

"Don't be such a pea-goose!" His words had snapped Alexandria from her weeping fit. "This is no time to be jumping to wrong conclusions. Our feelings, or lack of them, have nothing to say to anything. I asked you to come here because something quite dreadful has happened. And I should not have to remind you that you are the only family

I have left." And she forthwith poured out the story of the lost necklace.

Oliver was too stunned to speak at first. When he did regain his vocal powers, it was to say, "How could you, Alexandria, of all people, have been prevailed upon to take part in a game of hazard! Surely your own father's deplorable history should have been example enough—"

"Oliver!" she almost shrieked. "Pray do not read me a lecture. There is nothing you can possibly say about my folly that I have not already told myself at least a hundred times. What I want is for you to tell me what's to be done now."

Oliver clearly did not know. And Alexandria, as she watched the play of emotions upon his handsome face and saw distaste predominating, realized just how foolish her trust in him had been. Finally he said, "I really can't see that you have any other choice except to go to Harry and confess what has happened. From what you say, the necklace must be worth a small fortune. But Harry is plump enough in the pocket to stand the loss. And he, of all people, should be understanding of the kind of folly that caused you to lose it." His lip curled disdainfully.

"No, that is exactly what he will not understand," Alexandria retorted. "For it was not a mania for gambling that undid me. It was stupidity. Indeed, if I had not had such an aversion to hazard, I might have educated myself a bit and not stood there paying absolutely no attention to that—that—cursed wheel and allowed myself to be fleeced like a—a—perfect flat!" She had worked herself into quite a state. "And there's no use saying Harry will understand that." Her chin quivered. "For he won't. There's nobody quite as knowing as Harry is."

"No doubt you're right." Oliver looked at her in some alarm. "Don't cry, Alexandria. Even if he doesn't understand, I'm certain he'll forgive you."

"But I shall never be able to forgive myself," she wailed. "Please, Oliver, help me."

"I must say, Alexandria, what you ask is unreasonable. I really don't see what I can possibly do."

Alexandria had always thought that she admired Oliver for his levelheadedness. Now she found it merely irritating. She could not help but wish that the positions were reversed and it was Harry she was appealing to to extract her from some coil involving Oliver.

"One thing you could do," she said, "is to go to Lady Calcraft's establishment and look around. For all we really know, Roker could have been there every night running his devilish wheel. For Lady Calcraft has given strict orders not to admit Evelyn. But the doorman there won't know you."

"And just what am I supposed to do if Roker is there?" Oliver looked definitely alarmed. "From all you've said, the man is a common criminal and will stop at nothing."

"I don't know," she replied impatiently. "But we have to find him first, do we not? Then we can think of a plan."

Oliver's expression showed just what he thought of that bit of reasoning, but he picked up his gloves and began to put them on. "Then you will go? Oh, Oliver, I don't know how I can ever thank you."

"What for?" he answered crossly. "If you had come to me the moment you had lost the necklace, there might have been some point to this, though I doubt it. For I'm sure that villain left town for good the minute he got his hands on a fortune in diamonds. And if he should chance to be there, I don't know what I can do when I see him except place a wager on his wheel. Really, Alexandria, this is an insane business. And how I'm to explain my absence to Amelia is more than I can think of."

The fact that everything he was saying was clearly true didn't make it any more palatable to Alexandria. "I'm sorry to impose upon you, Oliver," she replied. "And you are right, of course. It's just that I can't give up till I'm sure there's no hope left. Then I shall tell Harry the whole truth. If you can locate Roker, then at least I can try to talk to him. Perhaps he hasn't disposed of the necklace. Maybe he and Lady Calcraft only want to get their revenge by throwing a scare into me."

Oliver gave her a pitying look. "You do realize, do you not, that I won't be able to go to that establishment before nine or ten o'clock?" She nodded miserably and he left. She resumed her tedious waiting.

When he finally returned, the clock had just struck twelve. During his absence her anxiety had reached the frenzied state. Nor did the sight of Oliver's agitation alleviate her fears.

"Oh, my God!" she exclaimed as he came bursting into the library, his face ashen while he gasped for breath. "Oh, my God," she repeated, "what has happened?"

"Can't talk yet," he panted. "Ran all the way."

"Oliver!" she shrieked. "If you don't tell me what has happened this very minute, I shall lose my mind!" and she ran to tug the bellpull furiously till the clapper's clamor reverberated through the house. The elderly Padgett was almost as breathless as Oliver when he arrived. "Quick, fetch Sir Oliver some brandy." This was no time to think of servants' gossip. Judging from Oliver's stricken look, tittle-tattle was the least of her concerns.

She did, however, snatch the tray from Padgett's hand when he delivered it and fairly pushed the curious butler out the door. "Now, for heaven's sake," she said after Oliver had had a deep gulp of the restorative, "tell me what has happened. Have you seen Mr. Roker?"

"No, I have not," Oliver replied with some asperity now that he had regained his breath. "I doubt he is even there. But I cannot say so with any assurance, for I did not get inside the place."

"You did not get inside! Then whatever—"

"Alexandria, if you will contrive to stop these hysterical outbursts, I shall try to tell you what occurred!" Oliver's glare was most unlover-like. "As I think I mentioned," he began, then paused to sip his brandy while Alexandria forced herself not to grab his lapels and shake him, "Amelia is not feeling quite the thing. So rather than—uh—distress her, I waited till she had gone to bed before I left the house. I had just reached the Calcraft residence and actually had my hand upon the knocker when the door burst open and I was almost trampled by two dozen or so patrons falling all over one another trying to flee the place." He paused for another sip.

"What was it?" she gasped. "Fire?"

"No, Henry. I did manage to stop one woman. The best I could gather from her hysterical babbling was that Henry had come bursting into the place looking for your Mr. Roker. Then there had been a terrible dust-up with that bruiser Maria Calcraft employs to rid the place of troublemakers and Henry had knocked the fellow out. After that, Lady Calcraft screamed for some of the men to band together and rush him, the woman said, and Henry pulled a pistol and threatened to blow off the head of the first person who took a step his way. That's when pandemonium set in and those people fled for their very lives, I gather, for the lady kept saying over and over, 'He's mad as King George—stark, raving mad!' At just that moment there was a shot followed by a terrible crash and the roulet wheel came flying right through the window. It's a wonder it did not kill someone." He shuddered. "Not to mention the danger of flying glass."

"Oh, my lord—what happened then?"

"Why, everybody ran, of course."

"You ran?" Alexandria looked at him in disbelief.

"Someone shouted, 'Here comes the watch!' By that time, you see, heads were sticking out of all the neighboring houses to see what was going on. And I'm sure someone had sent for help. For the Calcraft place is an unsavory element in a most respectable neighborhood, don't you know," he interjected with pursed lips. "The residents are demanding that it be closed."

"You mean you actually ran away?"

"I'm telling you, everybody ran. What did you expect me to do with the watch due to arrive at any moment? Who would believe that I was an innocent bystander and not one of the clients of that awful place? Think what being picked up by the watch would do to my political reputation—not to mention what Amelia would have to say about the matter." He shuddered at the thought.

"You heard a gunshot and then just ran off and

left your own cousin in that place without even knowing what had happened? Oh lord, I just know Harry's been killed and it's all my doing!" The hysterics she had been fending off all evening finally overtook her and she sank down on the sofa in a fit of weeping.

"There, there, now. No need to jump to rash conclusions. After all, Harry's the one who had the pistol. It's much more likely that he's shot someone else."

This did not have quite the comforting effect Oliver had intended, for Alexandria wept all the harder. He sat down beside her. "Please, Alexandria, control yourself. Here, have a sip of brandy." She took a gulp, hiccoughed, and the sobs subsided into quiet weeping. "There, there." He patted her shoulder awkwardly. "I'm sure all will turn out for the best."

The library door burst open. "Please don't disturb yourselves," Harry said between tight lips as they both leaped to their feet. "I only plan to be a moment."

It was horrifyingly obvious that he had been in quite a brawl. For all of Weston's careful tailoring, one blue superfine coat sleeve was ripped loose at the shoulder. His neck cloth was completely gone. His face was blood-streaked, with cuts above the eye and on the lip. Both eyelid and lip were now beginning to swell. And, to Alexandria the most frightening thing of all, the fierce light of combat still glistened in his eyes. Oliver took due note of this and prudently put the sofa between his cousin and himself. But Alexandria had run toward Harry before the fury in his face had stopped her cold.

"Oh, Harry, I feared you had been killed."

"As you see, I have not been so obliging. But if I had been, what did you propose to do about Amelia? Trust to luck that she'd die in childbirth?"

"Harry, don't talk like such a gudgeon. I can explain—"

"No doubt," he interrupted coldly, "but I haven't time to listen. I expect the watch momentarily. I merely stopped by to give you this." He shoved the jewel box into her hand. "May I suggest that you take better care of it from now on?" Before Alexandria could get her wits together and reply, he had left the room abruptly, slamming the door behind him.

This was to be a night that would keep the tongues wagging in the servants' hall for weeks. As Padgett was wont to say, "No sooner had the shock waves died down from the Honorable Henry letting himself out the front door in such a way as fair took it off its hinges, than the doorbell was set a-jangling by Master Evelyn. Then I'd no sooner reached me room and relit me pipe when his lordship himself was there demanding entrance."

When Evelyn burst into the room, Oliver had been saying a rather constrained farewell to Alexandria and there was that in his expression that spoke of disenchantment as he looked at his lost love. But if Alexandria even noticed, she certainly did not care.

"I say," Evelyn announced dramatically, "you won't believe what I just heard."

"Try us," Alexandria answered.

If he'd failed initially to create the dramatic suspense he'd hoped for, Evelyn was prepared to ignore it momentarily and build with narrative. He was delayed, however, from launching into his exposition by the arrival of Lord Woolridge.

As always, Alexandria could not help but be impressed by his lordship's cool detachment. What a perfect type to guide the ship of state, she thought admiringly as he surveyed the group with a half-smile and remarked dryly, "Well, I see I am not to be allowed to make my announcement. Tell me, though, have you seen my son?"

"He was just here, sir," Oliver volunteered. "To return this." He gestured toward the jewel case lying upon the sofa table.

"Oh, yes, the famous necklace." Lord Woolridge walked over and opened up the lid. The diamonds resting upon their bed of dark blue velvet came to dazzling life in the candlelight. Lord Woolridge gazed at them for a moment in complete silence. Then he shrugged and shut the lid. "This, as I understand, was the cause of Harry's sack of Calcraft House. I believe you lost the necklace playing roulet?"

Before Alexandria could frame an answer, Evelyn jumped into the breach. "It wasn't Alex's fault, sir. I'm to blame. I'm the one who insisted that we go there. Alex actually dislikes gambling, you see, sir, and is a perfect flat—not at all up to snuff—and really did not know she was being gulled until the thing was done. And of course she did not lose anything near the value of the diamonds anyhow, but the villain Roker wouldn't take her note and insisted she leave the necklace. And then he bolted with it. Actually, I still don't know how Harry—"

Alexandria decided it was time she spoke for herself and interrupted Evelyn's flow to say, "I'm terribly sorry, sir. What I did was unforgivable. No one can possibly reproach me the way I've reproached myself. I can well imagine what such an heirloom means to you."

"Heirloom?" Lord Woolridge's brows shot up.

"Yes. Harry had the diamonds reset for me. But they are the same stones that had been in your first wife's family for generations. I have been quite beside myself."

His lordship moved his lips in what he must have thought passed for a smile. "You had a perfect right to be disturbed over the monetary value of such a piece of jewelry. But I'm sorry you were agonizing over the other thing. I can assure you that my late wife possessed no family jewels. Henry obviously purchased these for you. Why he did not say so, I cannot imagine. But then, I've never pretended to understand any of his motives."

There was a moment of stunned silence as Alexandria's eyes opened wide and Oliver looked at her wonderingly.

"I still don't understand how he came to get them back." Evelyn was the first to recover from his lordship's bit of news. "Nobody mentioned that at Watier's. They said that—"

"First the Calcraft residence and then Watier's," his stepfather interposed. "You seem to be flying rather high, Evelyn."

"Not actually, sir." The young man colored. "I was merely a guest at Watier's and did not play, even though I was invited to sit in. Somehow I've been turned off hazard."

"That is the one piece of cheering news I've heard all evening," his lordship said.

"Actually, I came out a bit ahead at Maria Calcraft's," Evelyn went on defensively, "but, as I was going on to say," he continued, prudently shifting the conversation away from himself, "no one even mentioned the necklace in connection with Harry's—uh—activities at the gaming-house, so I don't think he found it there."

"Just what activities did they mention?" Harry's father asked with remarkable detachment. "I take it my son was the *on-dit* of the evening?"

"Oh, yes, sir. The place was set abuzz, in fact. You see, these two coves had come to Watier's straight from Calcraft's. As a matter of fact, they were saying that even before Harry wrecked the place they'd made up their minds not to go back there. The play was really insipid for the most part, they said. And, oh, Alex, they also said that cursed wheel was rigged up to stop wherever Roker wanted it!" Here Lord Woolridge cleared his throat. "But you're all waiting to hear what Harry did, are you not?"

"With bated breath," his stepfather replied.

"These coves said that Harry came to the door, but that this big bruiser Maria has guarding it wouldn't let him in. You should see that villain, sir." Evelyn's eyes sparkled with excitement. "Weighs a ton if he's a pound. Used to box professionally. Beat Savage Shelton himself once."

"We get the idea, Evelyn. Pray continue."

"Yes, sir. Maria had given orders that Harry not be allowed inside. She probably expected him after she sent that lock of hair, Alex. Anyway, they had this terrible dust-up in the entry hall with all the patrons leaning over the banisters and placing wagers on the outcome. Most of the money went against Harry, by the by, and Carlton—he's one of

214

the coves who told the story, don't you know—bet on him and made a killing."

Again Woolridge cleared his throat and Evelyn got back on course.

"Anyhow, Harry milled the bruiser down and went on up the stairs. But then the bloke got back on his feet somehow with his nose spouting blood like a Hyde Park fountain—sorry, Alex—and came up after Harry, and there was another terrible dust-up before Harry finally put out his lights.

"Then Harry demanded to know where Roker was, and when Maria wouldn't tell him, he pulled a gun. These coves said Maria had been screaming for help earlier, but she suddenly turned as cool as he was and said she wouldn't tell him even if she knew and that if Harry had been gulled he had it coming; besides, she knew perfectly well that he wouldn't shoot her. And he said that was true but that he would kill *this*! And he fired right into the wheel and then picked it up and sent it crashing through the window.

"The cove who was telling the story said that at this point some of the people thought Harry'd gone completely crazy and they started screaming and running out of there.

"But Maria just laughed at him and kind of sneered, 'Feel better now?' and Harry answered, 'Not particularly,' and said he didn't think he'd feel really good till he put her out of business and found Roker. And he went on to say that, while she was right, he couldn't shoot her to make her tell where Roker was, he'd just had a better idea. Since she was so free with her locks of hair, how would it be if he cut off the whole mess to remember her by. And he pulled out those scissors from the drawer and headed toward her, with her screaming bloody murder.

"She kept saying over and over that she really didn't know where Roker was and that, though she'd cooked up the plot to get Alexandria fleeced, the necklace business was pure happenstance and all Roker's doing—though fine with her, for all she ever wanted was to get back at Harry. At that point someone yelled, 'The watch is coming!' and everybody, including Harry, bolted, and those two chaps ended up at Watier's."

He paused for breath. "But I still don't know how Harry got the necklace back," he finished.

"I'm sure that, too, will make a dramatic recitation," Lord Woolridge commented. "If you find out, do number me among your audience, Evelyn."

Lord Woolridge almost absentmindedly opened the jewel box again and held up the necklace so that the diamonds caught the full power of the candelabra. "Lovely," he murmured. "Pity they are not heirlooms. Henry's mother would have sold her soul for them." He glanced away from the diamonds to see Alexandria staring at him curiously. "Don't be alarmed, my dear," he said, laying the necklace back into the box. "No need to stare so. I'm not at all light-fingered. You are in no danger of losing your jewels for a second time."

Alexandria felt her face grow red. "I was not even thinking of the necklace. I was looking at your ears," she said in some confusion.

"My ears!" Lord Woolridge looked astonished. "I think it's obvious, gentlemen, that we have kept Alexandria up far too long after the fatigues of the past few days. Evelyn, I think you should thank her for her many kindnesses during your London visit and say farewell. I do believe it's time for you to rusticate once more. I will not speak to your mother of your London adventures if you do not."

"Fair enough!" Evelyn's ready acquiescence seemed to take Lord Woolridge by surprise. His stepson grinned. "London's going to be quite flat anyhow without Harry, sir. I'd just as lief go home." He colored, then enveloped Alexandria in a big bear hug. "I'll miss you, though," he said.

"Will you walk with us, Oliver?" Lord Woolridge asked pointedly.

Oliver needed no prodding. He actually seemed eager to pick up his hat and cane. "Good night, Alexandria." He gave his cousin the stiffest of formal bows, which she did not even bother to acknowledge.

The front door had closed behind the trio before Alexandria recollected herself and went chasing after them down the marble steps. "Lord Woolridge, will you take the necklace for safekeeping?" she asked breathlessly.

"Certainly, if you wish." He looked at her curiously.

"I only hope some footpad doesn't knock us on the head for it before we get back to Brook Street," Evelyn remarked cheerfully. "That cursed necklace has caused enough trouble without that happening."

Alexandria stood quite still and watched their progress till they turned the corner out of sight. Then she sighed deeply and stepped back indoors.

"Shall I lock up now, ma'am?" Padgett was hovering in the background. "Or are you perhaps expecting still more visitors tonight?"

That was as close to sarcasm as Padgett had ever allowed himself to come.

Chapter Nineteen

THE FOLLOWING DAY ALEXANDRIA LEFT LONDON IN A hired postchaise. Her conscience twinged a bit at the extravagance, but she consoled herself that at least she had been less expensive to maintain than Harry's mistress. But then, neither had he gotten the same return on his investment that Miss Brady had given him. Still, she argued, the "Yellow Bounder," as those black-and-yellow vehicles were called, actually was a necessity. To prove her point, she had the coachman call at Pulteney's Hotel and kept him waiting for half an hour while she went inside.

Nor did she feel that the handsome sum she paid the driver to get her to Westmorland in three days' time was money wasted. At least, she justified it by telling herself that the news she was bringing Harry would be worth the expense to his peace of mind. Of course, there was a distinct possibility that Harry was not actually in Westmorland. And what she would do then did not bear thinking of. Nor, for that matter, did she know what she would do if she did find him there. She pushed the future resolutely from her mind and tried to enjoy the scenery she was passing through.

It was dusk when the chaise rolled between the stone gates of Gadsden Estate and started up the drive that circled for a mile to Gadsden House. But there was sufficient light remaining for Alexandria to see the well-tended park through which they drove and to gawk at its full complement of streams, shrubs, flowers, deer, and fowl.

She gasped aloud when they rounded a curve and the Palladian house just ahead of them burst into view. With its classic lines and pedimented portico, it could have been a temple on a Grecian isle. Only the stone of which the house was built looked truly English.

Alexandria tried not to allow herself to become intimidated as she climbed the marble steps and passed between the huge Corinthian columns to ring the front doorbell. She had, she thought, been well aware of Harry's wealth. But nothing had quite prepared her for all this.

The servant who answered spoke rather stiffly. "Yes, Mr. Romney is in residence; however, I think he has gone to the stables at the moment, miss."

"Which way are they?" she asked, and upon receiving their direction, requested that her luggage be taken from the chaise.

"Was Mr. Romney expecting you, miss?" the butler inquired, as tactfully as possible.

"Actually, I've arrived a bit sooner than he'd

thought," she extemporized. "But do pardon me. I should have mentioned that I am Mrs. Romney." As the butler's jaw dropped she ran back down the steps toward the stables.

For an instant, as they met on the narrow path halfway between the stables and the house, Alexandria thought Harry looked glad to see her. But it must have been a trick of the deceptive light, for his first words were not encouraging.

"What the devil are you doing here?"

"Looking for you, of course."

"You've found me, it appears." The Honorable Henry Romney punctuated this hostile statement with a sneeze.

Alexandria moved closer and peered at him in the fading light. "Oh, Harry, you look awful."

"Thank you," he retorted and blew his nose.

"Is it the grippe?" she asked solicitously.

"Of course not. Just a slight nasal irritation," he said impatiently.

"If that isn't just like a man, especially you, not to admit to—"

"Alexandria," he interrupted, "I do not think you drove all this distance to inquire about my health."

"Yes, in fact, I did, in part. Not that I knew you had the gr—whatever—but I was quite beside myself with worry when I heard you were going to look for that villain Roker. I had hoped to persuade you not to do such a reckless thing. Oh, Harry, I should never forgive myself if any harm came to you because of me."

Harry paused to sneeze again before replying. "Well, then, you might have saved yourself the journey and used the post. I could have told you in a letter that Roker has left England, probably for

220

France. Much as I'd enjoy drawing that bastard's cork, I'm not going to chase him all over the continent for the privilege. So you've had a trip for nothing."

"That is not the only reason I had to see you," she said with some asperity. "You should realize that I'm finding this interview very difficult. Please try not to be so quelling. Could we not walk a bit, instead of just standing on this path? After all, I've been in a chaise since dawn. And I'm getting a crick in my neck from staring up at you. Of course, if you do not feel up to it—" she added as an afterthought.

"Of course I'm up to it," he growled, beginning to stride back down the path in the direction from which he had come.

"Slow down!" his wife commanded.

"I thought you wanted exercise." He fairly raced across a wooden bridge that spanned a rapidly flowing stream, Alexandria on his heels.

"I want—I need—to talk to you. Oh, Harry, I cannot blame you for wishing me to the d-devil, but please let me try and explain."

He stopped and turned so abruptly that she almost collided with him. "Alexandria, let me warn you right now that if you start to blubber I shall throw you in the brook."

"I have no intention of doing such a thing."

"Good."

"Harry, stop!"

"Make up your mind, will you," he growled, leaning up against a tree.

"Harry, please let me try and explain how I lost the necklace. I never meant—"

"I never thought you did."

"It was the most lowering thing that has ever happened to me. After all the prosy things I'd said about your gambling, I lost more in the space of one half hour than you could have lost in—"

"I do not lose."

"You would have if you had played with Mr. Roker," she said defensively. "Evelyn said that the wheel was fixed to—"

"As anyone but a complete gudgeon would have known."

"You are determined to make this as difficult as possible, are you not? I suppose I cannot blame you. All I can do is repeat how terribly sorry I am."

"Alexandria, get one thing through your head. I don't give a tinker's damn about the necklace. And you were not totally to blame. I was the victim Maria Calcraft was after. You just happened to make her revenge easy by being so shatter-brained, that's all."

"I suppose I was," she retorted, "but it's unkind of you to say so when you do not even know the circumstances. I spent the entire time watching Evelyn instead of that devilish bouncing ball, wondering how I was to get him out of that female's clutches. It was the old man beside me who did all the punting. Of course had I known that Maria Calcraft was the woman you had sent all those locks of hair to, then I might have been on my guard. Really, Harry, I do not like her above half, but that was a shabby thing to do."

"Nothing is too shabby where she's concerned," was his curt answer. "Come on, let's walk."

It was growing dark by this time, but she stumbled after him. "What I don't understand is how you knew the necklace was gone in the first place or how you got it back."

"As to the former," he said dryly, "as soon as you and Evelyn made your little scene, the news spread all over London that Mrs. Romney, 'She's one of the Linnells—shocking gamesters, don't you know,'" he parroted, as she bit her tongue and longed to kick him, "that Mrs. Romney had lost a valuable necklace at roulet and that Maria Calcraft had sent me another lock of hair—which I've yet to see, though. Of course I heard the story. So did the pawnbroker that Roker sold it to. He brought it straight to me and I bought it back."

"Harry," she wailed. "What it must have cost you!"

"Not as much as it might have done. The broker made a profit, naturally. But he was more interested in building up future goodwill than in getting its true value."

"Harry, I am so sorry."

"I told you I don't give a damn about the necklace. Now could we change the subject?"

"Harry," she said diffidently, "could we not go back to the house? It's impossible to see you, which makes it hard to talk, and what I have to say next is rather—uh—delicate."

"More delicate than gambling away a fortune in diamonds?" he said with heavy sarcasm. "I can hardly wait."

They strode back to the house in awkward silence. Once, when Alexandria stumbled over a root in the darkness, Harry caught her around the waist and held her close to his side for a brief moment longer than seemed necessary. The strength of his grip and the warmth of his arm penetrating her several layers of clothing made her breath catch in her throat and her heart pound. But she had barely registered her own response when he pushed her none-too-gently away and strode off into the darkness. She struggled to keep pace. Apparently he was more out of charity with her than she had feared, which was very bad indeed.

The light from two pairs of sconces flanking convex mirrors on either side of the elegant entryway made Gadsden House seem a lot more warm and welcoming than its master. "A library is as good a place as any to receive bad news," he said. "Brooks, bring me some brandy in there, please." The butler had opened the door for them and Alexandria was conscious of other curious members of the staff lurking just out of sight.

"Brooks," Alexandria interposed with what she trusted was an ingratiating smile, "if there are any lemons, could you not have a hot punch prepared instead for Mr. Romney? It would be more medicinal, don't you agree?"

Now seen in the candlelight Harry did, indeed, look awful as he pulled out his rather appalling handkerchief to reapply it to his nose. His drawn face still showed signs of recent combat. And she was sure, as she looked him up and down from riding coat to buckskins to top boots, that he was thinner than when she'd seen him last.

"A very good suggestion, ma'am," the butler said approvingly. "And perhaps a supper for yourself?"

"Thank you very much, Brooks." She beamed back at the butler as Harry held the library door open for her to enter.

There was a brief wait while Alexandria removed her bonnet, using the gilt-framed mirror over the

Adam fireplace to pat her hair in place. Then she strolled about, gazing at the shelves of books that lined the walls while Harry sprawled in a wing chair by the empty fireplace and watched her with an expression she found hardly reassuring.

When the hot brandy punch had arrived, along with a cold collation and a glass of wine for Alexandria, and after the servants had withdrawn, Harry took a long draught of the steaming liquid. "Come, sit down," he said, indicating the chair opposite his where the tea tray had been set between them. "I'll fortify myself while you eat your supper. Then you can fire your salvo."

"I did not mean, when I said delicate, to imply that my news was bad," she told him through a bite of ham. "In fact, I believe you will be glad to hear it."

"Indeed?" Mr. Romney did not look convinced.

"I hardly know a proper way to lead up to this. So forgive me if I simply plunge right in. You see, on my way out of London I stopped by Pulteney's Hotel to see Colonel O'Hara. I asked him if it was true that he was your father and he said that most definitely he was not."

At this point the Honorable Henry Romney choked on his brandy punch. When he had quite recovered from his coughing fit, he stared at Alexandria incredulously.

"You see," she continued apologetically, "I had just noticed that Lord Woolridge's ears are exactly like your own, and really, if it were not for your broken nose, your profiles are quite similar. And, by the by, Colonel O'Hara says you also look very like your Irish grandfather." Alexandria noted that Harry seemed close to apoplexy and nipped this digression in the bud. "The thing was, you see, when I noted the similarity of the ears I thought it possible that you and Lord Woolridge had labored under a dreadful misapprehension for all these years. And so I decided to ask the colonel."

"And he denied it. How amazing," Harry sneered.

"I told him, of course," she continued calmly, "that there was no need for chivalry, for Lord Woolridge had informed me that Lady Woolridge had confessed to their affair. That really stunned the colonel." It seemed to stun Harry, too, though she refrained from commenting on it. "For you see, the whole thing came as a complete surprise. He'd never heard the rumors. He's been out of England for the most part, of course.

"I'm afraid then that Colonel O'Hara called your mother a few uncomplimentary names," Alexandria continued, "and said she'd been an unconscionable flirt, as well as a beauty without peer, and that she'd led him on until he was quite bedazzled. But she had stopped just short of going to bed with him, although he admitted trying his best to persuade her to do so. And, no, it would definitely not have slipped his mind, if that is what you're thinking. He said he was not such an accomplished rake as to forget any conquests, and that no man who met her could possibly forget your mother.

"Colonel O'Hara was of the opinion, though he did admit it might have come from conceit on his own part, that your mother was never unfaithful to your father. He said that, though she thrived on the attention she got from all the lovesick beaux dangling after her, she really was quite a high stickler in that respect. And as for telling Lord Woolridge what she did, well, the colonel's theory—he knew her quite well, you know; they were second cousins and had grown up together—was that she had the devil's own temper and likely wanted to get back at his lordship for something. Then she probably just forgot she'd ever said it. Colonel O'Hara went on to say that he could never understand why she married— forgive me, but these were his exact words—'a cold fish like Woolridge. He was devilish good-looking, of course, but not in her style. And no fortune to speak of.' I told him, of course, that she probably loved him, and he thought about it and agreed. 'Women get some funny maggots in their heads,' he told me, 'and Charles Romney, as he was then, was the only man who didn't actually grovel at Lydia's feet. His mind was always on politics, not on her. She probably,' he said, 'just told him his son wasn't really his to make him sit up and take notice. But, my God, what a damnable thing to do!' I'm quoting the colonel, of course," she added primly.

Harry still seemed unable to find his voice, so she continued. "At any rate, Colonel O'Hara promised me he'd go to see Lord Woolridge immediately and tell him the same thing he'd just told me."

Here Harry choked on his punch again. Suddenly his shoulders began to shake. "Oh, dear lord, I'd certainly give a monkey to hear that conversation," he finally managed to say.

"You think I did wrong then?" Alexandria sounded a bit aggrieved. She had not exactly expected gratitude, but still—

"No, I would not say that," he sputtered. "It's just—my God—it does take some getting used to, you marching up to O'Hara and accusing him of adultery, then him haring off to my father to deny

227

it all." He went off once again into spasms of choked laughter.

"I think you've had entirely too much punch," she said with asperity, "though it does seem to have done wonders for your grippe. Do you realize you have not sneezed in quite some time? Perhaps tomorrow you may see what I've just told you in a different light and be quite glad of it."

"I am now," he answered almost solemnly. "It's just so damned ridiculous." And he practically rolled off his chair with laughter.

"Really, Harry, I do not see how we can talk seriously if you cannot control yourself."

"You mean there's more?"

"Of course there's more. We have to decide what's to be done about our marriage."

That seemed to sober him up immediately. "Yes, I thought you'd get around to that."

"Of course you know that our marriage can be annulled." Since he was not looking at her, he did not see the misery on her face.

"Of course. But Oliver would have a bit more difficulty in proving his had not been consummated."

She raised her eyebrows in surprise.

"Why on earth would Oliver wish to do such a thing? And what does Oliver have to say to our situation?"

"What indeed?" His lip curled. "I can see no other reason for your sudden desire for freedom. But, as I pointed out, Oliver can hardly marry you."

"Marry Oliver! I would not marry Oliver if he were the last man alive!" Alexandria's observation, while hardly original, seemed to carry the ring of truth. Harry stared at her intently.

"Since when?" he asked.

"Since—oh, for heaven's sake, I don't know when. Forever, it seems now, and certainly since he went running off from Lady Calcraft's gaming parlor after there'd been a pistol shot and that wheel had crashed through the window and he did not know if you were alive or dead. Of all the cowardly, ramshackle things—"

"Oliver did that, did he?" Harry grinned. "You can hardly blame him. There's been little love lost between the two of us."

"I most certainly can blame him! You are cousins. And don't try to bamboozle me into thinking you'd do the same if the positions were reversed, for I'll not believe you."

"Just the same, Alex"— Harry sobered up again— "it's hard for me to believe you're not still in love with him. He was always at Grosvenor Square when I chanced to come there. I found you in his arms just the other night. After you, so you've just said, were supposedly angry with him because he abandoned me to my fate." It was obvious Harry was far from convinced of her disenchantment.

"I was not in his arms," she retorted. "I was having the hysterics because he'd heard that shot and I was afraid you'd been killed and he was trying to bring me around and I was wishing he was in Jericho. And that so-called assignation was to get him to help me find that odious necklace. I do not mean, of course, that it is odious," she amended. "It's the trouble it caused that I refer to. The necklace is the most lovely thing I've ever seen and I still do not understand how you came to buy it. But, as I was saying, I needed Oliver's help, for I had no one else to turn to. Though I must say he certainly proved to be a grave disappointment."

"You might have come to me," Harry remarked.

"And have you throw it up to me for the rest of my life that I lost it gaming? Not if I could help it," she retorted vehemently.

"You think I would do that?" His look was injured innocence. "Damme, but you're right. But forgive me," he went on after a moment's thought. "I'm sure it's not your fault, but I'm still confused. If you've no desire for Oliver, why this rush to end our marriage?"

"For your sake, of course. I want to give you back your freedom."

"My sake? Shouldn't I be the one to make that decision? I was not aware that I had lost my freedom."

"If you're not aware, you can't have thought. I knew, of course, when you first proposed that it was a maggoty notion from your point of view. But I fear I wound up thinking chiefly of myself. And, to be quite honest, I never could have imagined that it would turn out as badly for you as it did. I had anticipated that you'd wish to marry someone else. But you yourself discounted that notion, remember?" He nodded solemnly. "But I never anticipated that I'd start off by acting like a fishwife when you began our elopement late, though, as I explained, that was simply a nervous reaction because I feared you would not come. But the really terrible thing I did was to break up your card game on our wedding night. You must have thought of that when you learned I'd gambled away your necklace."

"It did cross my mind." He grinned.

"And the results were that I landed you in a brawl, and hit you with that japanned candlestick myself, and made you an archenemy. After that, I cost you I don't even want to think how much money to maintain me. And then I evidently caused you to quarrel and finish with Miss Brady. But still you did not return to Grosvenor Square. And all of this was even before the awful episode of the necklace." She wound up her recitation with a groan.

"Summed up like that, I really have had an eventful married life."

"Yes, and you received absolutely no benefit." His eyebrows shot up, and her face went red. "I mean, of course, that neither your position in society nor your strained relations with your father have improved."

"You forget the matchmaking mamas, however," he interposed solemnly. "There was a definite halt in all their efforts."

"I am glad. But on balance, that seems rather small. So I'm offering you your freedom."

"And I'm rejecting it."

"You can't. There's no need to carry chivalry that far. If you're thinking I cannot obtain another position, I'm sure I can. It would not surprise me at all if Lady Augusta wished me back. So do not allow chivalry—"

"I am never chivalrous," he interrupted.

"You are too! It was chivalrous of you to tell Arabel Fielding that Banbury Tale about having a *tendre* for me in order to atone for the slight you gave her."

"That was no Banbury Tale."

"Of course it was. You are not going to say you offered for me on that account. It will not wash."

He seemed to be thinking carefully. "No, that was not precisely why I offered for you."

"Why did you, then?"

"I warn you, you will not like it."

"Tell me."

"Because I felt sorry for you." Her eyes flashed in indignation and he held up his hand to stop the reply forming on her lips. "All right, then, perhaps saying I felt sorry for you isn't quite accurate. To be more precise, it made me furious to find that fiery, proud, adorable little girl who'd had at me with a stick in defense of her pudding-hearted hero"— he grinned as she glared at him—"looking so pathetically downtrodden and placed in such a humiliating position. At first I was ready to horsewhip Oliver and duck old Augusta in the horse trough, but on balance it made more sense to run off with you."

"You are chivalrous then," she commented without enthusiasm.

"I thought so too at first," he answered cheerfully. "Till it occurred to me that I'd been around put-upon companions all my life and had never before felt the slightest urge to rush to their rescue. Then I had to admit to myself that I most likely had a *tendre* for you. After that lowering realization, confessing to Lady Arabel was child's play."

"Are you sure you did not confuse that emotion with jealousy? I'm convinced you mainly wished to score off Oliver."

"If that were true, I'd have taken the first Lady Fielding from him. The loss of her fortune would have hurt him far more than the loss of you."

"That's all too true," she answered dismally. "How I ever could have admired him defies belief."

"Not at all. He's devilishly good-looking. Let's give the man his due."

"I suppose so," she said doubtfully, "though I no longer admire his type at all."

"Please don't tell my father," Harry murmured, but she failed to note his comment as she mulled over what she'd just said.

"I think I most certainly was drawn to him as a child because he was so—well—beautiful. I admired that sort of thing back then. But I cannot find it particularly becoming in a man."

"How encouraging!"

"But to get back to the point we were discussing, if you did truly, which I do not believe for one moment, care for me, why did you simply not come out and say so?"

"A man's entitled to some pride. You were besotted over Oliver. Besides, I've just admitted I did not sort out my motives until much later."

"But you avoided me so. I had thought—wondered—that time you kissed me. And at the Frost Fair. Did you know that the day at the Frost Fair was by far the nicest day I have ever spent?"

"You did say so. But I was not sure you meant it."

"And I thought then that you rather . . . liked me . . . but afterwards you avoided me more than ever. Why did you not return to Grosvenor Square after you and Miss Brady parted?"

"That's easy to answer. I feared I'd come home foxed some night and kick in your bedchamber door and climb into bed with you. And I had given you my word in that department."

"Oh," she whispered. Then, after a long pause while he looked at her and she gazed at the bit of

233

fringe she was twisting on her paisley shawl, she asked, "How do we go on now?"

"Well," he answered, "I can only tell you what I intend to do."

"And what is that?"

"Stay here and get on with the new agricultural methods that you told my father I'm so taken with. I have no desire to return to London for a bit. In fact, I'm *persona non grata* there, I expect, after wrecking Maria's gambling hell.

"You, of course, must do as you think best," he added. "It's only fair to warn you, however, that Brooks will have put your things into my room. And that the maid will by now have put your nightdress on my bed. So, if you do decide to stay, it will needs be as my wife."

"But what are your wishes in the matter?" she asked timidly.

His eyes held hers for a moment. Then he stood and yawned and stretched elaborately. "To go to bed."

"I am rather fatigued myself," she answered primly.

"That, Mrs. Romney, is a pity," he rejoined, drawing her into his arms and kissing her soundly.

The long-delayed Romney honeymoon was most idyllic. Only one thing marred the romantic interlude. Exactly one day after she'd arrived at Gadsden House, Mrs. Romney succumbed to an acute case of the grippe and was forced to remain in bed three days in order to be finally rid of it. The fact that Mr. Romney found it necessary to attend his wife constantly behind closed doors did not go unnoticed by the servants.